ROSCOE WENT NORTH...

But he got no farther than Colorado. There, in a little cowtown bar, he met a man named Tad Burnham, a skinny scarecrow of a man with a dolorous pockmarked face, who struck up a conversation with Roscoe and after a few drinks said:

"Banks, eh? Wouldn't be related to Hal Banks that was killed in Wyoming in '92, would you? You look like him."

"Yes," Roscoe said. "He was my father."

"Did you know my father?" he asked.

Burnham sipped at his glass of whiskey.

"In a way," he said. "I was there when they killed him. There was no mistake," Burnham said evenly. "They knew just what they were doing. The bastards!"

As Roscoe looked at his profile the thin lips began to move and the whining voice told the story that Roscoe dreaded to hear.

Books by William Decker

The Holdouts
To Be a Man

Published by POCKET BOOKS

TO BE A MAN

WILLIAM DECKER

PUBLISHED BY POCKET BOOKS NEW YORK

POCKET BOOKS, a Simon & Schuster division of
GULF & WESTERN CORPORATION
1230 Avenue of the Americas, New York, N.Y. 10020

For Bruce and Pamela

To be a man is, precisely, to be responsible.

—Antoine de Saint-Exupéry,
Wind, Sand and Stars

PART

1

<My name is Roscoe. Roscoe Banks. When I was little they called me Button, but that was a long time ago. Most things nowadays seem like they happened a long time ago.>

Chapter 1

IT WAS APRIL. Spring nudged winter north across the prairie the way a wise old cow steadily noses her new-born calf out into the sunlight from the thicket where it was born. But winter would not be hurried and stopped often to ice the water holes and freeze the manured ground around the hayracks. It was tiresome to young Roscoe Banks. He had had enough of the long Montana winter, the cold, the bulky clothes, and chores that were a part of the season. As he filled the woodbox he was using all the skill he had developed in his eight years to lay the twisted sticks and split chunks in the box so that they took up as much room as possible without being too obvious. His father, Hal Banks, and his "Uncle" Jim Phillips were scraping a fresh hide on the ground beside the low log building which served as a barn. Roscoe passed them on his trips from the woodpile to the kitchen.

Hal Banks was a tall man with a thick shock of coarse brown hair, a long face with irregular features, a resolutely jutting jaw, and a nose that had obviously been broken more than once. Despite his broad shoulders he appeared to be a slab-sided lightweight beside Jim Phillips, who was big and beefy. Both men's faces were weathered and lined around the eyes and mouth from squinting against the sun and dust and snow glare. Both had the steady, intent gaze and faded blue eyes of plainsmen. Roscoe practiced the squint and the look, but since there was no mirror he was never sure of the effect.

Stepping out of the cabin for another trip to the wood-pile, Roscoe looked up toward the pass and saw four horsemen coming down from the higher ranges which surrounded the basin. He called to Hal and Jim, who straightened from their work to look in the direction he was pointing. Mary Phillips stepped to the doorway, wiping her hands on her apron. She smiled at Roscoe and lifted one hand to shade her eyes as she looked toward the pass where the boy was pointing. She was a slight, energetic woman with a wealth of auburn hair which Roscoe admired.

"Well," she said, resting a hand on Roscoe's shoulder, "I believe we're going to have some company, Button."

The two men came across the yard to stand with Roscoe and Mary to watch the riders wind down from the rocky ridge through the occasional ancient junipers which grew aslant, showing the force and persistence of the prevailing winds. Roscoe was excited and curious, but since his father seemed to be taking the event calmly he restrained himself. He met Mary's glance and her deep brown eyes showed excitement. The boy smiled quickly at her. She turned back into the cabin and he heard the crash of stove lids.

With Mary gone it seemed to Roscoe that the atmosphere changed from happy expectancy to ominous anticipation. Hal and Jim watched the slope intently even though the riders had disappeared into the pines above the meadow. Something about the steady way the horsemen approached and the drawn expression around his father's mouth made Roscoe uneasy. Nothing was said, and when one of the saddle horses in the corral let out an unexpected cough the boy flinched. He stood as tall as he could beside the two men, and while it suited him to be with them, he had to suppress a longing for Mary to come and back him up. He wanted to leave the woman's world of the kitchen, but was not quite ready to close the door behind himself.

After an uncomfortable wait the four riders appeared in the meadow and started across the flat toward the buildings. Roscoe was just able to make out the color of the horses at that distance and was surprised when Hal said tersely, "Bar X men," almost under his breath.

"Wouldn't surprise me," Jim said. "They've been moving a lot of stock up to the high range. Started just as soon as the snow was off. Cow herd, from what I've seen. They turned some of those Hereford bulls in with them. Button and I saw a couple when we were scouting around last week before you came up."

Roscoe remembered that just a few days before his father had appeared on one of his sporadic visits Jim had taken him on a long ride into the high country ostensibly to study range and water conditions, but the boy had felt that the trip had something to do with the fact that the Bar X syndicate had shown signs of taking over the mountain grazing. He had seen the short-legged red bulls with white faces which Jim had called Herefords. They were chunky little things, not half as big as the roan Oregon-bred bull Jim had traded for two years ago. Since they were not as big Roscoe could not see their value, because naturally the bigger you could grow your cattle the better. But Jim seemed to think that they were the coming thing. He said that five years ago Herefords were rare but now they were getting commoner.

As they rode home that evening in the fading light Jim talked on the way he always did about the business side of raising cattle, and Roscoe listened, but with only half the attention he showed when Hal talked about the mean horses and wild cattle he worked with.

"I've an idea," Jim had said, "you'll live to see a time when the rangy Texas cattle are hard to find. They don't do well here in Montana. The Oregon cattle are good keepers and they turn out a fine big side of beef, but those Herefords look like they're more steak than soup meat."

Roscoe was not convinced. Their big roan bull seemed to him everything that a bull should be. He stood as tall as Roscoe's Indian pony, Chopo, and he weighed over a ton. His massive head, bulging jaws, and truculent amber eyes reminded the boy of a lynx cat he had met face to face in the mountains once. The awesome aspects of the ugly animal seemed appropriate to him; fitting attributes for a herd sire and boss of the range.

*   *   *

"They're from the Bar X all right," Hal said suddenly, startling Roscoe. "That one on the big gray is Hank Henry or I miss my bet."

The four riders came on directly across the level meadow, their horses abreast. Clusters of cattle lay around the fringe of the flat, rhythmically chewing their cuds. The cattle watched the horsemen briefly and then returned to their chewing, their noses tipped slightly upward, their eyes closed, and their front legs tucked under their briskets.

Roscoe forgot his fear as he studied the men riding into the yard. He watched the straight-legged way they sat their saddles and the fluid grace two of them showed as their spooky mounts skittered snorting away from the scent of the fresh hide. One of the ponies, a bay with a bald face, bounded sideways with an agile leap that took him halfway across the yard, and Roscoe was careful to note that the rider remained deep in his saddle with no apparent effort. The man on the big gray, the one Hal had called Hank Henry, reined toward Hal and Jim. He seemed to notice that their sleeves were turned back and their hands bloody, and he glanced quickly toward the hide. The handsome deep-chested horse, so much like the others Roscoe had seen brought back from Oregon, merely arched his neck gracefully and blew one rolling snort toward the half-cleaned cowhide.

Roscoe stayed where he was in the doorway as his father and Jim stepped forward to meet the mounted men. He was so intent that he did not realize Mary was beside him until he felt her hand on his shoulder. He glanced up quickly, trying to read her face. She was smiling. Roscoe saw that she had changed her apron and brushed her handsome hair into a fresh halo of curls. Reassured, he turned his attention to the men in the yard.

"Get down," Jim said loudly. "Get down. Come in and eat."

It was nowhere near time to eat, Roscoe knew, but this was what you always said to visitors.

"No, Phillips," Henry said, drawing rein and steadying

the gray with a hand on its neck. "We can't take the time."

Jim protested as he moved across the yard toward the riders, saying that there was food aplenty, and pointing at the fresh hide. Roscoe noticed that he kicked back a corner of the hide casually but hard enough to show the brand. The boy looked to the right where his father stood hipshot and apparently relaxed, and then to the left at the three other horsemen. From spurs to Stetsons he took them in and memorized each detail for the day when he would be putting together an outfit of his own. Two of the men rode typically wiry little Texas cow ponies and wore the southern-style bat-winged caps. The third was mounted on a stout northern bronc and wore the angora leggings some called "shotguns." All of them lolled with elaborate ease in their saddles, and one of the southerners even had a leg crooked around his saddle horn sitting sidesaddle.

Roscoe was startled out of his concentrated study by Hank Henry saying brusquely:

"No, we got to make tracks back to the wagon. We're moving cows up above. Brought some more Hereford bulls up this morning and thought we'd better stop by and tell you we don't want no roan calves next year. Best you keep that shorthorn of yours out of the high country."

The boy watched his father as Hal lifted his head suddenly to stare at Henry and then look in turn at each of the riders lounging in their saddles behind the foreman. Roscoe heard Mary draw in a quick breath and felt her hand tighten on his shoulder as Hal straightened and took a step forward.

"You could have saved yourself the trip, Henry," Hal said evenly. "We've got breeding aplenty for him here at home."

"Fine," the foreman said. "Glad to hear it 'cause if he comes visiting we'll make an ox out of him."

He lifted his reins and swung the gray easily on its hocks to take him out of the yard in a striding road gait. Roscoe watched the way the others worked from the hips to draw their horses back and around in one gesture and jog away after Henry. He looked back to Hal and Jim, who were watching the riders wind down the trail that led out of the basin. Jim's face showed concern, but Roscoe knew from Hal's expression that his father was very near one of his uncontrollable outbursts of rage which terrified the boy.

"Highhanded bastard," was all Hal said.

"More wood, Button," Mary called from the cabin, but Roscoe did not move at once. He was watching the four riders from the Bar X growing smaller and smaller as they moved down the trail. He was relieved that they were gone, but very excited over having seen them. What had it all been about? The way Hal's face had tightened up meant trouble for sure. How about the way that bald-faced pony spooked. And the power in that big gray. The riders vanished and Roscoe turned reluctantly toward the stack of wood. He inspected his father and Jim as he passed them. Hal was just right, but Jim was too big. Hal looked as if he belonged horseback, incomplete afoot. Jim seemed natural afoot and nothing seemed to hang on him right. The two were talking and Roscoe stopped to listen.

"You may not think so," Hal was saying heatedly, "but I've seen what happens. I've worked for the likes of them and seen their dirty doings."

"Forget it," Jim said, shaking his head. "We've got grass enough for our stock down here, and if they want to run on the mountain they won't be hurting us."

"Maybeso," Hal said, "but the pressure's on big spreads like that. They're hurting. When the time comes they figure they need this basin along with the high range, they'll ace you right out."

"Hard to do, seeing as how we got title to the land."

"Hard, hell!" Hal barked. "You know as well as I do how they operate. They'll run you out, or burn you out, or scare you out."

"I don't scare so easy," Jim said quietly. "Besides we've got law now. Nowadays there's more of us little fellows than the big ones and we've got courts to settle trouble."

"So what?" Hal said. "It wouldn't be much of a trick for them to burn our iron on a couple of their calves and convince the court you're a rustler. They've done it before. That and worse."

"People around here know me better," Jim said, "and they'd be sitting on the jury."

Hal shook his head, and Jim looked away toward the mountains.

"Hal," Jim said slowly, "are you worried about those yearlings you brought up here this trip?"

"Hell, no," Hal answered quickly. "They're clean. Besides, they came from a long way off."

Roscoe moved away toward the woodpile, confused by what he had heard but sure of one thing—the Bar X represented a threat. He looked toward the mountains and imagined the trails and meadows crawling with riders like the four who had just left the yard. He felt very vulnerable in the open basin. Instead of carrying in more wood he wandered out by the barn and sat behind the stack of wild hay where he often went to be alone. Sitting in a pocket he had hollowed in the stack, he puzzled over the situation. Start at the beginning, he told himself. Start at the very beginning and go over it and maybe it will add up.

The beginning for Roscoe lay in the stories he occasionally badgered his father into telling when Hal made one of his infrequent visits to the ranch where Roscoe had lived with Jim and Mary as long as he could remember. He remembered riding home with Hal one evening when they paused on a grassy knoll and sat for a long time simply taking in the scene. Roscoe was glad to rest. As the cool shadow of the western hills crept across the softly rolling glasslands in the meadow they watched the cattle begin to hump themselves to their feet one by one and graze. The cattle thrust out their long tongues to wrap in tufts of grass and jerked each mouthful up with quick swings of the head. As far as they would see the range was a soft, rich green dotted with blocky roan cattle.

"Now you take these Oregon Durhams," Hal said, gesturing. "Who would've thought we'd see the likes of them?"

"How do you mean?" Roscoe said, hoping for a story.

"Well, Button, when I first came to this country nobody ever heard of Oregon cattle. The farmers and all that went through here years before on their way west had milk cows and the like. Mostly Shorthorns. But they didn't settle here and the range belonged to the buffalo when I first saw it. I came behind a herd of Texas Longhorns. '77 it was. They'd just signed a new treaty with the Sioux and Cheyennes over at the Red Cloud Agency the year before and opened up this country to cattle. We drove them all the way from Texas and they trailed like saddle horses, those Longhorns, strung out and striding, and a man wanted to be well mounted to stay with them."

Roscoe saw in his mind's eye long winding herds dragging columns of dust in their wake.

"Why did they come, Dad?" he asked. "Why bring them up here?"

Hal turned from scanning the basin and looked intently at his son. He locked both hands on the horn of his saddle and leaned forward hunching his powerful shoulders.

"Well, now," he said, "that's a long story. Let's start away back and see can we wade through it. When your grandpa came home from the War Between the States I guess there wasn't much to come home to. Virginia was pretty well used up and he took a big notion to go somewhere else. Your grandpa was a man that didn't mess around once he made his mind up to something, so he wasn't long in making his move. I was just a pup then, younger than you, but I can remember the trip. Us five kids, Aunt Lucy, Ma and Pa, and two niggers that couldn't get it through their heads that since the war Pa wasn't obliged to look out for them. It was a trip, I'll tell you, and when we got there it didn't look like we'd bettered ourselves by much. But Pa, he set to and went right to farming like he thought it would just naturally work. There was trouble right off with Indians and trouble right along with weather."

"Tell about the Indians," Roscoe interrupted.

"Oh, now, I've told and told about them," Hal said with a grin. "I'm just warming up to tell about the cattle. Don't go shouldering me off the trail.

"Following a mule was never cut so it fit me. Nor the hoeing that came after. But I was sixteen before I took off for good and all. There was an outfit holding a cow hunt north of where we lived and I joined up with them. Let me tell you, in those days gathering cattle was like rounding up so many deer. Well, when we had made a herd the boss comes along and says anybody that wants can stay on to drive them north. That just suited me so I went along.

"Now about why there were so many cattle, and why they went north, that worked like this. Everybody was gone for so long during the war that the stock just took to the brush and nobody bothered them. With the war over, the folks up north in the east got to shopping around for beef and the Texans took to driving their wild cattle up to where they could sell them. Pretty quick the railroads came to meet them and the next thing you know the easterners got so used to the idea of having beef that they started getting particular about what kind of beef. Like I said, those Longhorns could test the wind of any pony that ever wore hair, and they were so tough you couldn't get a fork in the gravy. So this business of fattening them on grass started. We'd camp out with a herd until fall and get them sleek, ship them, and head for Texas for more.

"Pretty quick some halfway permanent camps got established and some cow herds were brought up to be held here and calved out. But those thin-skinned Texican cattle never did do good up here with the cold and all, so some started bringing the Oregon cattle in. Sure, there are plenty of Texas cattle left, but they're being bred out by the Durhams and Herefords. Most of the Longhorns got wiped out in the Big Die-up in '86."

"Tell about that," Roscoe said breathlessly and shivered at the memory of the story he had heard often before.

The story was still fresh in the minds of the cattlemen and one that they told each other with endless embellishments as if reminding one another that it could happen again at any time. An early spring, a dry summer, a freak snowstorm, were enough to set the ranchers squinting at the northern horizon and grimly anticipating the worst. The spring of 1886 had come early and with it the beginning of a long drouth. Hal and Jim drove their cattle up to the summer range and cleared the low grasslands to save them for winter feed. Without rain the lower plains quickly lost their spring color as a yellow hue crept in, erasing the green. By the end of June the range was dry and the grass seed shattered, springs and creeks began drying up. Hal and Jim rode through the long, hot days trying to hold the cattle on the upper range.

Each day they could see the clouds of dust far to the south and the west which marked more herds being driven into the already heavily stocked country. The market was exceptionally low, and many cattle which ordinarily would have gone to slaughter were being held over in the hope that prices would improve. Hal scouted the area and learned from one of the trail outfits that the North Platte River was crowded with cattle all the way down to its junction with the South Platte and that herds were being held along all the tributaries.

The trails from the south were bare of grass, and from Fort Laramie to the Bozeman Trail, in the Lander Valley and Wind River country, the grass was gone and there were too many cattle.

Still the dust clouds filled the sky, meaning more cattle on the way. Hal and Jim watched their stock eat up the winter feed in August. When the time came to ship the steers they found that the market had settled to $1.80 per hundredweight and the steers were in poor shape. Other ranchers drove to the railroad, shipped their steers, and found that the animals did not bring enough to pay the freight bill. Cold weather set in early.

An old Gros Ventre Indian rode up to their corrals one bitter afternoon early in November. He was swathed in blankets and his scrawny pony humped around away from the wind when the old man dismounted. Hal and Jim knew him and invited him to the cabin where Mary was fixing supper. He stood by the fire, erect, wrinkled, and thin; his face so marked by time as to seem ageless.

The old man predicted a storm and Hal squinted toward the north where clouds the color of wood smoke were banked above the hills. After accepting some tobacco the ancient Indian began a long story involving his personal history and the histories of his family and tribe. His voice took on a singsong chant as he told of listening to his grandfather recount the days long before the white men came, the days when buffalo blackened the plains for weeks at a time as they moved south early in the year.

All the familiar animals had vanished that year and the storms had come early. Climbing out of their drifted dwellings, the Indians found little on their hunts, but they did see things none of them had ever seen before: huge white owls and black foxes. Great numbers of the tribe died in the long, brutal winter. The white owls and black foxes were never seen again. Surely they had been the spirits of death.

Here the old man drew himself up, adjusting his robes, and paused dramatically.

"Yesterday," he said, "I saw three white owls."

He clamped his toothless gums tightly shut and thrust out his jaw. Jim shook his head to show that he was properly impressed. After condescending to accept some more tobacco, the old Indian went out into the rising wind. They watched him ride away, bowed against the blast, and then turned back to the fire.

"What do you make of that?" Mary asked.

"The story?" Jim said.

"Yes."

"Oh, it's just another tribal legend. Probably like the story of the flood in the Bible. They've taken all the rough winters there ever were and rolled them up into one."

"Yes, but those owls."

"Oh," Jim said, "they likely got driven down here out of the far north by the bad winter. Ran out of food up there and drifted farther south than usual."

"But he says he saw some yesterday."

"Hell," Hal said, "if there'd been snakes in the story he'd have seen them too."

"I don't like it just the same," Mary said, turning to the stove.

"Well, don't let that old fool throw a scare into you," Hal grumbled.

The wind grew stronger as the sun lowered, and even in the tight little cabin cold began to creep across the floor. Hal and Jim went out to complete their chores before supper, bundling into their saddle coats.

On his way back to the cabin with a huge armload of wood, Hal heard a sudden chorus of squawks go up from the shed where the chickens roosted. Dropping the wood, he raced to the door of the log barn and jerked his saddle gun from its scabbard. As he ran back out into the first swirl of snowflakes he levered a shell into the chamber.

Rounding the corner of the barn, he saw something streak away from the chicken shed with a hen slung across its back. Hal stopped and swung the gun up. The sights leveled and as they swept past the blurred target he mashed the trigger. KA-WOW, the shot roared and then wow, wow, wow, came the echoes as the animal leaped and fell twitching on the bare ground. Jim came stumbling out of the barn and Mary called from the cabin door, "Jim! Jim?"

Hal passed the body of the dead hen and toed over the furry heap beside it. It was one of the biggest foxes he had ever seen. Nearly as big as a wolf, and coal black.

"It's all right," he called back to Mary. "Just a fox in the chickens."

He and Jim dragged the animals to the manure pile and buried them. They decided against mentioning the color of the fox to Mary and after gathering up the wood Hal had dropped they returned to the cabin. Little Roscoe was swinging his spoon against an empty tin plate, shouting, "Bang, bang, bang." Hal grinned at him. Outside it began to snow harder.

In the morning they awoke to find that over six inches of snow covered the range. It had stopped falling but the slate-gray sky looked heavy with snow. Hal and Jim rode all that day locating their cattle and trying to move them back toward their range. They struggled through drifts and beat their numbed hands against their chaps as the temperature fell steadily. That night they returned cold and discouraged, sure that they would be unable to market any of the steers that year.

Snow fell steadily for the next two days and they fought harder trying to hold the cattle from drifting ahead of the storm. Cows and calves, steers and bulls moved before the driving snow like a fleet of small boats. Hal and Jim exhausted themselves and their horses floundering through stirrup-deep drifts in the two-below cold. When the skies cleared they found the cattle badly scattered.

Another bad storm moved in on the eighth of December, bringing more snow and a piercing wind which blew for three days and brought the temperature down to twelve below, where it stayed until the eighteenth. Then the sun came out briefly to reveal a few humped-up emaciated cows. On the ninth of January another savage gale swept down from the northwest. Sixteen inches of snow fell and the mercury dropped to twenty-seven below on the twelfth, thirty below on the fourteenth, and forty-six below on the fifteenth.

More snow. The arctic circle seemed to have moved down on them and they were helpless. They tried driving their small band of saddle horses up the draws and canyons where the cattle huddled, seeking shelter. The horses broke through the snow to let the cattle search for whatever scanty feed might be left. Hal found cows eating willow branches as thick as buggy whips and chewing each other's manes and tails.

February saw more snow and then a sudden chinook. The warm wind came up without warning and thawed the white blanket covering the prairie. But before it could accomplish much the chinook was swept away like a memory of summer by a blast of bitter arctic air which froze the slush into solid, impenetrable ice.

Now even the saddle horses could not paw through the icy crust. The strongest steers began to die and at night the willow trees exploded like pistol shots as the sap froze in them. A parade of gaunt cattle drifted by the cabin, their hooves squeaking on the ice, blood frozen on their hocks, chins, and nostrils. Gently they began to lower themselves to the ice, one by one, and as the raw wind ruffled the shaggy hair on their bony hips they died. They moaned protests as Hal and Jim struggled trying to tail them up. There was no fight left in them. It was almost as if the cattle had forgotten that there had ever been anything else in life except snow, cold, and starvation.

That was the end of it. When spring finally came and the thaws began only a handful of cattle remained, and most of them were crippled. Carcasses lined the canyons and drift fences and were piled against the riverbanks. Stinking, bloated bodies hung high in trees which had been drifted over by snow. The buzzards, wolves, and coyotes thrived and grew fat.

Jim began making plans for fencing meadows, storing hay, and building up another herd. Hal shook his head, saying it was too slow a process. Leaving Roscoe with Jim and Mary, he rode south to find a quicker method. Ever since then he had worked for the big outfits which had survived. He came back only occasionally, and sometimes when he came he was driving a little bunch of young stock to be branded and turned in with the growing herd. He always explained that they were part of his wages or the results of bets.

And really this was all that Roscoe knew. He knew it by talks with Jim, questions he asked Mary, and, most important of all, the precious times when he managed to start Hal talking. Now, sitting in the hollowed haystack taking comfort from the imagined security of his hiding place and from the tepid April sun, he was confused.

Running beneath his uncertainty, blunting his curiosity, was a warning, a hint that insinuated that perhaps he did not want to find the answers. He thought about the Bar X men instead, twitching his small shoulders as he recalled the way they reined their horses.

That night in his bed Roscoe went over the details of the visitors. By concentrating on not thinking about the threatening atmosphere surrounding the incident he managed to isolate the details he wanted without scaring himself. One by one he cataloged the precise tilt of a spur, the wrist action of a gloved hand holding reins, exactly how a lariat was spooled and hung. By now the men were faceless, impersonal, and Roscoe was about to slip off to sleep when his father raised his voice in the kitchen below him and Roscoe came wide-awake. He seldom paid any attention to the grownups' conversation, but tonight he peeked down through a crack in the rough flooring of the loft above the kitchen and listened.

HAL: Maybe it's not as bad as I make out, but that Hank Henry rubs me the wrong way. I know him. We've butted heads a couple of times and I haven't backed up from him yet.

JIM: There's nothing wrong with backing up once in a while.

HAL: Well, I don't back worth a damn. Specially from a four-flusher like Henry. I've got no more use for him than a hog has for a sidesaddle.

MARY: Don't go looking for trouble, Hal. You might find it. We live here, you know. We don't want to get involved in anything that can be avoided.

HAL: I know. I won't start anything. In a couple of weeks I'll have to be heading south. I'm supposed to meet Diek Harlow in Buffalo and go partners with him on a deal. I know what you mean. But that Henry needs some manners taught him all the same.

MARY: Yes, but let him get his lessons somewhere else.

JIM: The Bar X can't shake us. You know how we set. Ever since your Peg died and we put our places together we've worked toward one idea: to build a ranch that is complete in itself. We've done pretty well by adding to it and improving it. What's more, we own it. We probably own more land than the Bar X. This free range is getting scarcer every year, and the time is coming when the big boys are going to have to own or lease land.

HAL: Maybeso, but you don't want to go underestimating outfits like the Bar X. They're in a bind and they're going to bull their way out. You don't want to be standing in the road or you're likely to get run over. You don't see much of it up here, but I know what's going on, and let me tell you, it's building up to storm. I don't want to be out in the middle of it when the storm breaks. That's why I'm going in on this deal with Dick. We'll be filling government beef contracts and there won't be any call for us to get mixed up in the fight that's sure to come.

MARY: You ought to marry again, Hal. Roscoe needs you and a mother. Jim and I have tried and we don't think he's unhappy, but he needs more.

HAL: No. I doubt it. You and Jim are more mother and father to him than he's ever apt to find. Besides, in my book a man only marries once. I'll take him off one day and make a hand of him.

MARY: Why?

HAL: Why?

MARY: Yes. Why do you want to teach him something that's already dead? Save some money and send him away for an education. You and Jim have seen the changes and should know that by the time he's grown there won't be much left of the old ways. There's no sense in bringing him up to be something that's already out of date. You might just as well raise him to be a buffalo hunter.

HAL: There's a lot of good in what we learned.

JIM: Mary's right, Hal. The whole thing's changing. Knowing what we do is getting less and less important. Beef is sold by the pound now, not by the head. It's more of a business.

HAL: I wasn't thinking of the cow business so much. It was more like making a man of him. Teaching him how to handle things that test his wind. Showing him what his word is worth.

MARY: You don't have to make a saddle tramp out of him to do that.

JIM: Now, Mary, a little bit of cowboying won't hurt the boy any. Besides, that's a long way off.

A long way off, Roscoe thought. Not so long. Soon. He slept and dreamed himself tall and well mounted, riding beside his father.

Chapter 2

ROSCOE WAS OUT beside the barn practicing a backhand toss that he had seen his father use to catch his saddle horse. He had the biggest chunk of firewood he could find out on the dry ground away from the barn and he threw the loop over and over, without much success. He wished that Hal would come and give him lessons, but on second thought he decided that it was just as well that Hal was not around. The day before, driven by some impulse he did not understand, Roscoe had, quite deliberately, hit the milk cow with a rock as she paused for a drink on the way in to be milked. It had startled the cow so that she jumped into the pond and arrived at the barn with heavy mud all over her bag and no intention of letting down her milk. Hal's face had gone dark with rage and he shouted curses at the boy, who kept well out of his way knowing that if he could reach him Hal would hit him.

But Roscoe also knew that if he stayed out of Hal's sight soon his father would forget his anger and be very gentle and kind to make up for his rage. It was nearly time for Hal to be leaving and Roscoe knew that this too would soften him and make him more fun to be with. That was why he was not surprised when Hal, obviously looking for him, found him by the barn and said, "Saddle up, son."

The boy ran to the pasture and went through the elaborate ritual it always required to catch his spotted Indian pony Chopo. The little horse knew that he would eventually succumb to the temptation of the grain, but at first he always acted as though his pride was so great that he would not let gluttony interfere with his freedom. Usually Roscoe resigned himself to Chopo's feigned determination to remain at large, knowing that if he simply stood still and rattled the grain in the bucket the little horse would finally come slavering to heel. Today Roscoe was impatient, anxious to be off with Hal, hoping to redeem himself. He allowed Chopo only one wild dash out across the pasture and then he turned, as if in disgust, and started for the corral. Chopo was obviously upset by this unexpected denial of his customary face-saving maneuvers. Whinnying frantically he beat Roscoe to the corral.

Chopo cranked his short-haired, almost ratty tail as Roscoe led him to the corral fence so that the saddle could be dragged down from the top rail onto the spotted pony's back. The little horse drew his legs up under his stubby body and swelled as the boy threaded the latigo through the cinch rings. Hal smiled as he watched Roscoe alternately tug at the strap and punch the pony's distended belly. Gradually, an inch at a time, the boy managed to take up the slack while Chopo shook his oversized head up and down in protest. Once the pony reached back as if to take a nip at Roscoe, and Hal laughed aloud as his son elbowed the gray muzzle without letting go of the latigo and gained several inches on the soft leather strap.

They rode out of the yard together with Roscoe standing in his stirrups imitating Hal's posture. Mary stood in the cabin doorway smiling as they passed, but Roscoe stared straight ahead, sternly studying the mountains.

It was a long, comfortable ride punctuated by pauses and sudden bursts of conversation from Hal. Roscoe did not stop to be puzzled by his father's unusual loquacious mood, he was enjoying it too much to be bothered with trying to explain it. Hal seemed to be trying to tell him something, something important, and Roscoe was not sure he understood.

Once when they were moving slowly up a trail wide enough for them to ride side by side, Hal told an exciting story about a remarkably mean horse that he had been assigned. After describing dozens of ways the bronc had tried to kill or cripple him Hal wound up praising the horse. Roscoe shook his head, saying he thought the horse ought to be shot.

"Now just you wait a minute," Hal said. "That pony was mean, but he was tough. You could pull wet saddle blankets off him night after night, and even though he shied a kick at you when you did it, you knew you could put the saddle back on him and ride all night. He was mean, but he was honest. Like a lot of men I know. If you know them you know what you can count on from them. Don't be too quick judging a man. Before I ever had call to use a razor I knew that a man might have done some pretty bad things and still be the best kind of help in a tight spot."

They rode on and Roscoe pondered the meaning of what Hal had said. At times when Hal talked this way it confused and frightened Roscoe. Something Hal had told him a year earlier caused a recurrent nightmare involving stampeding cattle and mangled men. Roscoe remembered word for word what Hal had said:

"I'll tell you something else, Button. Don't ever bring the things that really matter to you down inside out in the open. You don't know what I'm talking about now, but you'll come to. What you really feel about something is secret. Keep it that way. If you don't you'll never be able to do a lot of things that have to be done sometimes. Like when a friend, and I mean a good friend that you've gone through all kinds of particular hell with, is lying there all busted up begging for your gun. You know there's nobody in a hundred miles that could do him any good. You've got to be able to pass him your gun and to try not to listen to the shot and not to think of anything. Then go on, and later pay no attention to the slobs that want you to get teary-eyed over dogs they lost when they were kids. Life may leave room for some to cry over lost dogs, but the way we are we can't even cry over our friends. I know. I've buried too many of them."

What had he meant, "the way we are"? Roscoe was afraid to ask.

There were so many questions he wanted to ask his father, but some fear kept him silent. When Hal was gone Roscoe carried on imaginary conversations with him about everything under the sun, but in his presence the boy was nervous and apprehensive. It was all he could do to answer simple questions and encourage Hal to talk.

The clear blue sky began gradually to lose its brightness, and the smell of night came on with the shadows. Roscoe was hungry, but it had been such a fine afternoon with his father in that peaceful, friendly mood that he did not want to let it end.

"Time we were looking for the feed bag," Hal said.

"Yeah," Roscoe answered, trying to sound older than eight, "my stomach's beginning to think my throat was cut."

Hal smiled down at the serious-faced youngster, and they turned their horses toward home. Then suddenly he checked his horse and stared intently across the basin toward a trail which led down from the pastures on the mountain. Roscoe tried to see what it might be that his father was studying. He watched the lines around Hal's weathered face tighten.

"There's something about the way that bull's moving I don't like," Hal said.

He kneed his horse into a lope out across the floor of the basin. Roscoe stirred Chopo into a run, and his hunger was forgotten in the excitement. They reined in their horses at the foot of the mountain trail and watched the big roan bull plod methodically toward them.

Roscoe saw that his right horn was broken at the base

and dangled down along the jawbone. Blood matted the hair on that side of his face. The big animal came steadily on, moaning and mumbling low in his chest. When he hit the flat abreast of them, he looked at the two riders and blinked his ugly yellow eyes, tipped his nose up, and gave a long, high-pitched bugle.

"Looks like he came out second best in a fight with one of the Bar X bulls," Roscoe said, trying to sound very knowing and adult.

Hal leaned on his saddle horn and said nothing. The bull turned and ambled toward the cattle on the flat, wringing his tail as he went. Hal straightened abruptly in the saddle, causing his horse to shy a few dancing steps.

"The sonsabitches," he said. "The goddam sonsabitches."

Then Roscoe saw that the insides of the bull's hind legs were covered with dried blood and that his bag was gone. He realized that the bull had been cut, and he remembered Hank Henry sitting proud on the big gray horse and saying, "We'll make an ox out of him." The horn had probably been broken when they roped him to do the job.

"How stout is that lass rope of yours?" Hal asked quietly as he looked up the trail to the mountain meadows.

"My rope?" Roscoe said. "It's a good one."

"Lemme see."

"It's real stout," Roscoe said, "pretty near new."

"Maybe so," Hal said, "but I better see all the same. You been dragging in wood with it and all."

Roscoe handed over the coiled rope and watched Hal run it through his hands looking to see if it was stranded or worn. He handed the rope back and dismounted.

"Better check your cinch on that blow-bellied bastard," Hal said, drawing up his latigo, "so your saddle won't turn."

"What are we going to rope?" Roscoe wanted to know.

"A bull," Hal said, stepping back up onto his horse, "a whiteface bull."

He turned his horse up the trail the roan bull had just

come down and started off fast. Roscoe urged little Chopo along behind, holding the horn and standing in his stirrups trying to keep up. The shadows had stretched all the way across the basin and had started up the slope they were climbing, but it was still daylight on the top. They hurried up the steadily rising broken ground.

Roscoe was kept so busy pushing along behind his father that he hardly noticed that they plunged into the cool darkness of a patch of pines and out into a bright green meadow and up another steep slope beyond. He began to get a pain in his side from the pounding trot. When it seemed that he could go no further he shifted his weight to one leg and hung on, gasping for breath. He did not know how far they had climbed, but a glance over his shoulder once showed him the dark basin far below like a puddle of rain water.

When they came to the edge of another of the abrupt meadows, Hal stopped and sat his horse looking toward the woods on the other side of the grassy flat. Roscoe did not need to rein Chopo in. There were many cattle strung out across the shadowy clearing, and as the boy's thumping heart gradually slowed he watched Hal studying them.

"Best check your cinch again," Hal said as he swung to the ground.

Roscoe's legs nearly buckled as he slid to the ground, but he hung onto the stirrup and caught himself. Once back in the saddle he watched Hal shake out a loop in his rope and then tie the other end hard and fast to his saddle horn. Roscoe began to do the same.

"No," Hal said. "Don't tie yours on. Here's what we'll do. There's one of those Hereford bulls over near where that little spur of trees sticks out on the other side. We'll work around downwind from him and see if we can get the jump on him. He's not too big. A three-year-old, I judge. I'm going to take a whack at busting him. You come right along behind, and if I can't jerk him over I'll holler and you come up and heel him. If I do bust him, you come in and catch his hind legs after he goes down. O.K.?"

Roscoe nodded as he arranged the coils of rope in his rein hand and the loop in his right. He was so excited that he could not trust his voice. His heart was pounding again, but it was not because he was out of breath.

Hal turned his horse and Roscoe followed as they rode through the trees skirting the clearing. They crossed a narrow creek at the lower end of the meadow and worked their way toward the finger of trees that stuck out where the cattle were. Now and then they had to detour around a thicket or windfall. Once a low branch hit Roscoe a stinging blow across the cheek.

Finally Hal held up his right hand and they stopped. He looked back at Roscoe and pointed toward the clearing. Roscoe could not see anything, but he nodded. Hal leaned forward, and his horse shot out of the woods. Roscoe followed.

The cattle threw up their heads and scattered as the two riders crashed out of the cover. Roscoe was so intent on sticking with his father that he could not take time to look for the bull. Little Chopo stretched out his neck and ran for all he was worth as the boy leaned over the saddle horn. Roscoe saw Hal's arm go up.

The loop whirled once, twice, three times, and then the arm went down and forward. The pace did not slacken, but as Roscoe watched Hal's horse veered slightly to the left. That horse has done this before, Roscoe was thinking. As the horse moved over Roscoe could see the humped-up, running bull ahead and saw that the loop had been drawn up tight around the base of the blocky animal's horns.

Still at a dead run, Hal stood in his stirrups and flipped his rope so that it ran from the bull's horns along the far side of its body and then back to Hal's saddle horn. Hal swung his weight onto his left stirrup and reined his galloping horse sharply out to the left.

Roscoe lost all sense of speed as they flew along. He carried his reins and the coils of his rope in his left hand while he held the loop shoulder high in his right. He saw the rope coming back from the bull's horns tighten just at the animal's hocks as Hal hit the end of the slack going away to the left. The bull's head jerked suddenly to the right, and the rope lifted his hind legs up under him.

Hal was standing in his left stirrup now, twisted and looking back as he rode away. The bull flipped completely over and came down with a thud flat on its back with its head twisted awkwardly toward its hindquarters. Roscoe swung out sharply to avoid running over the stunned animal.

"Put it on him," Hal shouted, and Roscoe saw that his father had his horse backed hard against the rope, stretching it taut. Trembling, the boy rode toward the bull's hind feet which were limply thrust straight up in the air. He swung his loop and tossed but hit the ground six feet away from the bull.

"Take your time," Hal said evenly. "Ride in close."

Roscoe spooled his rope and tossed again. This time he hit the hind legs but had to juggle the loop on.

"Dally down and ride away," Hal called, and Roscoe frantically wrapped his rope around the saddle horn as he made Chopo tighten the slack. Once the seemingly inert bull's hind legs were stretched out, Hal rode to the animal's head and quickly dismounted.

Kneeling on the heavy neck, he took the loop off the bull's horns and slipped it around the thick front legs. With a wave of his hand, he sent his horse running backward until it hit the end of the rope tied to the saddle horn and then the well-trained horse squatted on his hindquarters, drawing the bull's legs out straight. Hal rose from the ground and looked at the two horses and the straight line of ropes between them. Satisfied, he dug into his pants pocket and brought out a heavy jackknife.

"O.K.," Hal said, "make that goat lean a little."

Roscoe tugged at his reins, and Chopo staggered back against the tight rope. The boy watched as his father drew the knife down the bull's shinbone in two quick slashes. After a moment he saw Hal peel a strip of hide off the bull's stubby leg. The animal had gotten his head straightened and let out a high-pitched bellow as he waved his horns and tugged helplessly against the ropes.

Hal drew the bull's white tasseled tail between its hind

legs and rolled the animal farther over on its back. He took the strip of hide he had cut from the bull's leg and tied it around the flesh-colored bag as high and as tight as he could. When he seemed satisfied that the hide was drawn as tightly as possible, he knotted it and trimmed the loose ends.

"Now, damn you," Hal said, rising to his feet, "let's see how many of your calves the Bar X ever gets to brand."

He walked back to his horse and swung easily up into the saddle.

"O.K.," he called, "ride to him."

Roscoe thumped his heels against's Chopo's sides, and both horses moved in toward the bull. Hal had to lean down and lash the tail of his rope across the bull's face before the animal would make an effort to rise. Then, struggling and scrambling, the bull spread the slack loops and gained his feet to dash away. The ropes dropped to the ground, and Roscoe spooled his up to tie it to his saddle.

Hal sat his horse and watched the bull gallop clumsily up the meadow where the other cattle had gathered to watch.

"I'd like to doctor a couple more," Hal said, "but it's getting too dark."

They turned their horses and began the long descent toward home. Roscoe began to tremble and told himself it was the chilly air that caused it. Hal stopped once and let the boy come abreast of him.

"You did just right, son," he said. "A man couldn't ask for better help."

Roscoe grinned and clenched his chattering teeth.

"Hell," Hal said, looking at the boy. "Best we head for the fire. You're shaking like a dog passing peach seeds."

Jim met them in the dark meadow above the cabin.

"Thought maybe you and the boy were holding off a couple of thousand Injuns," he said. "Figured I'd come see the fight."

He and Hal rode together, talking as they made their

way to the corrals. Roscoe, suddenly completely exhausted, had all he could do to stay in the saddle, but a wild elation fought the fatigue and he sang silently over and over: "A man couldn't ask for better help. A man couldn't ask for better help."

Chapter 3

ROSCOE ATE QUICKLY and climbed the ladder to his bed in the loft above the kitchen before Hal and Jim came in from the barn. He was too numb with fatigue to even try to tell Mary what had happened. She did not press him with questions, but as he settled into his blankets he heard her talking with the men below. He did not listen, he was too busy happily remembering how the bull had looked as it flipped in the air on the end of his father's rope, how he felt when Chopo strained back against his taut lariat, the shivering excitement, and Hal's praise.

He slid gently into sleep and dreamed the episode over and over with many complications. He and Hal were in a meadow crowded with bulls and it seemed that they must rope them all. As fast as they caught one several more appeared. They rode frantically, roped desperately, but they could not keep up. Mary and Jim stood at the edge of the clearing, scolding, but Hal never so much as glanced in their direction. Roscoe looked back toward them often, but felt compelled to follow his father's furious chase. He wanted to go over and explain to Mary that they were only doing what was right, but Hal called to him and he raced off. They chased a bull into the woods and when they came out in the clearing again Roscoe could see that it was their own big roan bull galloping along clumsily with his broken horn flopping horribly

and blood gushing from his groin. Roscoe tried to shout
a warning to Hal, but no sound would come. Hal roped
the bull and rode away but when the big animal hit the
ground it seemed to disintegrate and Hal was left with
nothing but a flapping empty hide on the end of his rope.
The four Bar X riders appeared at the edge of the timber
laughing derisively, rocking in their saddles. Hal chased
them into the woods and Roscoe was left alone in the
meadow. He turned back toward Jim and Mary, but they
had vanished.

A few days later Hal put his gear together. Roscoe
busied himself trying to help, pretending that he was
going off with Hal. Eventually they were through. One
horse was saddled and a second carried Hal's bedroll,
which had his belongings folded inside. Hal turned to
Jim.

"I'm sorry Mary had to get upset," he said.

"She'll get over it," Jim answered.

"Maybe it was a damnfool thing to do, but when I saw
they'd cut that bull I was mortal mad."

"I'd of likely done the same," Jim said.

"They make thieves and outlaws of us," Hal said, looking toward the mountains. "Those big outfits are so used
to having their own way they think they can ride a man
down. When they make a gather they pick up everything
on the range, but when anybody else goes to brand or
ship they come poking around telling you you can't make
a move till the stock's inspected. They go around trying
to tell you what you can and can't do. Maybe it's like
Mary says, but I get riled."

"She'll simmer down," Jim said.

"She thinks it'll make trouble, but like as not they
won't notice it. That hide will shrink as it dries and take
his balls off neat. He won't bleed. They'll see it sooner
or later but probably not for some time," Hal said. "Anyhow, they got more bulls."

They both stood silent for a while. Jim squatted and
began tracing designs in the dirt with a stick.

"That Hank Henry needs some manners taught him,"

Hal said. "But, like Mary says, it wouldn't do to get the
whole Bar X down on you. I might just run into him
sometime."

"Forget it."

Roscoe had sidled up to his father and was studying
the smooth walnut grips on the Colt which hung at the
tall man's right hip in a brush-scarred holster. He looked
at the gun and the thick, stubby cartridges in the soft
leather belt above it. The pistol looked so solid, the grips
so smooth. Without willing himself to do so, Roscoe
slowly raised his hand until his fingers touched the gun
butt and curved around it.

Hal went on talking, and the boy stood there with the
handle of the gun clenched in his fist. It was comfortable
and somehow gave him a feeling of strength and power.
He felt that this would be a good thing to have, a fine
thing to hold at night when he lay on the straw pallet in
the loft alone saying the long, involved prayers in which
he bargained and traded with God. A gun like this would
be a comfort.

Hal let out a long-drawn, "Well," and Roscoe let go
of the pistol just as the lean flank turned away. He
watched the easy way the gun hung as it was carried away
toward the waiting horses and he followed, looking not
so much at his father as at the darkened walnut grips.
Hal untied his pack horse, gathered his reins, and laid a
hand on Roscoe's shoulder.

"You behave, Button," he said, and Roscoe nodded,
looking down and holding back tears. "I'll likely see you
in the fall."

With that he stepped up into the saddle and started out
of the yard.

"Take care," Jim said. And then Hal was gone.

Less than a month later word came back that Hal and
his partner Dick Harlow had been killed at their camp
near Buffalo by an army of ranchers and hired gunmen
who suspected them of rustling. The Johnson County
War was on.

Jim rode to town for more complete news and re-

turned two days later with all the information he could
gather. He told Roscoe that it had been a case of mistaken identity. Mary comforted the boy as much as she
could and Jim went to great lengths to take his mind off
his loss, but they were only partially successful. Roscoe
went through his chores as he always had, but he took to
spending more and more of his time riding out alone.
He set up a collection of figure-four traps around the
range and used them as an excuse for his rides. He
caught a wide variety of birds and small animals in the
box traps which were triggered by slotted sticks, but he
usually let the captives go after he had examined them.
One day he returned to the meadow where he and Hal
had roped the Hereford bull. He had not planned to go
that far into the mountains, but once on the trail he
simply kept going until he found what he thought was
the same field and he tried to imagine what the scene
would have looked like to an observer at the edge of the
timber. He called up an image of Hal, broad-shouldered
and supple on a big bronc racing across the flat. The
image rode toward him and slid the wild-eyed horse to
a square stop at his side and, smiling broadly, Hal raised
a hand in salute and let it come to rest on Roscoe's
scrawny shoulder. "A man couldn't ask for better help,"
the daydream said and Roscoe wept.

Hiccuping sobs and with hot tears burning his eyes,
the boy turned his horse away from the meadow and
started home. He went back to the meadow twice that
summer and cried each time. These were the only times
he let himself weep and by fall he felt that he could
face the meadow dry-eyed, but then he was too busy
helping Jim with the cattle to ride up the mountain. The
Bar X sent a crew into the mountain and gathered their
cattle to drive them south to winter range. Roscoe and
Jim saw some of the riders at a distance, but none of
them visited the cabin. Roscoe wondered if they had
discovered the bull. He and Jim herded their cattle close
while the Bar X cleaned the upper range and, although
Jim seemed his usual placid self, Roscoe noted the way

the big man could not keep from scanning the high country.

As Roscoe grew older he thought more and more about his father so that as the actual memories gradually faded they were replaced by impressions of his own creation. The boy remembered Hal Banks as a tall figure on horseback who rode into and out of his life at intervals. He gradually forgot that he was strangely uncomfortable during Hal's visits and that after Hal left everything seemed somehow more relaxed.

Jim and Mary never roared at him for a mistake the way Hal did. They never heaped his plate with more food than he could possibly eat and then insisted that he clean it up. They did not give him jobs that were far beyond his abilities so that he came almost to expect to fail.

"It's because he loves you so," Mary had said once, trying to console the boy after one such episode. "He wants you to be the best in the world. You're his son, and he expects more of you than he does anyone else."

But at such times Roscoe wanted his father to be like Jim, who was easygoing, who smiled so often, who seemed never in a hurry.

Between visits from his father Roscoe would forget his unhappiness and imagine Hal bossing a crew on some faraway ranch, riding the toughest broncs and roping wild cattle. Jim, who handled axes and pitchforks more than he did a rope, who rode the same gentle old horses all the time, who took orders from Mary, seemed pale by comparison. Jim never discouraged the boy from romanticizing his father. He told him all the stories he could remember about Hal's prowess with horses, ropes, and guns.

He told Roscoe all that he knew about Hal's past and how Hal had married and homesteaded the quarter section adjacent to Jim's. He described Roscoe's mother and told him what he could of her death "from some kind of a fever" when the boy was two years old. It was then that Jim and Mary had persuaded Hal to move in with them and at the same time they consolidated their ranges and herds. Then had come the killing winter of '86 and afterwards Hal had more or less turned his back on the ranch and had ridden off to find work where he could. Once he had been sent west to Baker City, Oregon, in charge of a crew of fifteen men with orders to buy and drive back a herd of eighteen hundred head. He did the job in record time and when he had delivered the cattle to the rancher up on the Musselshell River he came home to tell Jim and Mary of the opportunity he had discovered. At that time cattle could be bought in Oregon at prices ranging from twelve to eighteen dollars a head when they were worth thirty-five to forty dollars in Cheyenne and it only cost about a dollar each to drive them back. That was how he and Jim had rebuilt their herd. But Hal had never settled down. He always came home with money or cattle but he could never make himself stay long. .

In time the boy had built an image of Hal Banks which stood for everything he held admirable. Everything else was forgotten, and the boy set out to become what he imagined his father had been, imitating a myth. Even the account of Hal's death was distorted until Roscoe really believed that his father had been killed by mistake, that the Invaders had not known who was in the cabin they fired. Jim could never bring himself to even consider that perhaps Hal had been a thief.

Both Jim and Mary did their best for the boy. As he grew older they tried to draw him along toward life with sanity and good judgment. Mary did what she could toward his formal education, and Jim tried to impress upon him his theories of progressive ranching. They both encouraged his veneration of the "old days" but pointed out the inevitable changes brought on by progress.

And since Roscoe felt that they were somehow belittling his ideals, he determined to worship the idols of the past even more fervently. He turned more and more within himself, and while he submitted to their guidance superficially, beneath the surface he grew more and more romantic and reactionary. His daydreams of the future took on more and more aspects of the past.

By the time he reached fifteen Roscoe felt that he had learned all that he could from Jim about ranching. Each year it seemed that Jim was moving farther and farther in a direction that Roscoe did not want to go. More fences were strung, more meadows hayed, more stock kept in during the winter.

The winter days became an almost continuous round of chores from the first milking in the morning to the last one at night. Every morning it was the same: Jim's hand tugging gently at his shoulder, waking him in the frosty darkness. Roscoe would stumble to the kitchen to dress by the stove. Milk and feed, wood and water. In his sleepy mind the seemingly perpetual jobs lay ahead like a series of hurdles between himself and the warm blankets which he had just vacated. He had no patience with the scheme of measuring out life by chores and seasons.

One morning as he began his daily winter routine the idea of leaving, of going out on his own, stepped boldly out of the back of his mind where it had been undergoing incubation. He was leaning his cheek against the cow's warm flank as his hands pumped steadily at her teats, drawing jets of creamy milk. He was not yet fully awake and entertained the idea vaguely in a dreamlike state which did not require that he be very realistic. The milk streamed into the bucket with a regular purr, raising a head of foam as he pictured himself and the details of his outfit as he rode among men. The cow interrupted his reverie by splattering the soggy brush of her tail against the side of his face. Roscoe cursed and drew his sleeve across his cheek. Milk and butter are good alright, he thought, but I'd sure be willing to do without.

When he was through milking he turned the cow out and forked down some hay for the saddle horses. Hefting the foamy bucket, he started toward the house, trudging through the deep powdery snow. The bucket steamed faintly in the sharp morning air. He saw Jim coming up the slope from the big hay stack, lifting his feet high, leaving tracks that looked as if they had been made by some ice age monster. Jim's bulky clothing exaggerated his considerable size, and his snow-encrusted mittens resembled white boxing gloves.

Roscoe set the milk bucket inside the outer door and proceeded to kick and stamp the snow from his clumsy cowhide overshoes. He stripped off the overshoes, his mackinaw, mittens, and cap and went into the warm kitchen thinking of what he could replace each of these articles with when he was out on his own. There would be high-heeled boots, a full-length buffalo hide saddle coat split nearly to the waist for riding, horsehide gloves a man could handle a rope with, and a felt hat of beaver fur with a wide brim and high crown. He would wear the crown undented as his father had.

"Your face is dirty," Mary said, smiling as she took the milk bucket from him.

Just after his sixteenth birthday Roscoe announced his decision to strike out on his own and was surprised when both Jim and Mary seemed prepared for the move. They discussed his plans objectively and Roscoe, who had been building up his nerve for the announcement for weeks, was deflated by the easy way they accepted the idea. Quickly, before they changed their minds, he moved up his departure date and began to gather his gear together.

The night before he left, Jim called him from the corrals where he had been going over his outfit for the last time. Roscoe came into the warm kitchen which was so familiar. Jim, sitting at the plank table in the soft orange light of a kerosene lamp, suddenly appeared to Roscoe older and tired. The lines drooping down from his nose to the corners of his mouth seemed deeper, sadder. Roscoe started to regret that he was leaving, to wonder who Jim would get to help him, but at the sight of what Jim had on the table Roscoe swept all regrets out of his mind.

There in the lamplight lay a long-barreled single-action Colt with worn walnut grips. The pistol was in a well-oiled holster which had been stained and scarred by weather and brush. Roscoe knew at once that he had last seen that gun and holster eight years before on the day that he had said his last goodbye to his father. His right hand tightened automatically as he recalled the solid grip of the pistol.

"Sit down," Jim said gently.

Roscoe dragged up a chair and sat down. He stared at the pistol and felt a great eagerness to pick it up.

"Bill Reeves gave me this after your dad was killed," Jim said, laying one of his big, rough-knuckled hands on the gun. "It was Hal's. Bill was one of them that came along later and buried him, and he brought this along with that sack of stuff there."

Jim gestured at a canvas bag on the floor, and Roscoe managed to look at the bag but came quickly back to the gun.

"It's his spurs and such plunder," Jim went on. "I've saved it all because I figured it would be good for you to have. You won't need the gun the way your dad did, this is 1900, but the time might come when it would be handy."

Jim shoved the gun, holster and cartridge belt across the table toward him, and Roscoe reached out eagerly. The smooth, solid grips molded themselves in his palm.

"Now you'll likely get away early and we won't have time for much talk so I wanted to get my say tonight. I'm not going to try to talk you out of leaving. I think it's a good thing for you to go take a look around. But I want you to get one thing set in the back of your head. Half of this place is yours, and me and Mary are just going to take care of it for you till you come back.

"I know that right now you can't see this place at all. Nobody can blame you for wanting to get out and around a little. You wouldn't be normal if you didn't. You want to go where they don't spend half their time callousing their butts on mower seats or irrigating or feeding hay, and that's natural. You want to ride out in the morning with a crew of good men on snuffy broncs and handle big herds. I know the feel of it. Your dad and I did our share.

"The difference is that when your dad and I got ready to settle down there was still good land like this basin that a man could claim and prove up on. Now the good free land is mostly gone.

"But you go ride your broncs and chase your wild cattle. Be free as you like. But when you start waking up tired in the morning, when you catch yourself hoping that your pony won't buck, when you see a light way off in some cabin and wish you were in by the fire; then you come on home."

Roscoe blinked rapidly and looked down at the canvas sack on the floor. His Adam's apple seemed to be swelling and he doubted if he could speak.

The next morning he left and felt guilty because he was so happy to be leaving. Riding one horse and leading another with his bed and belongings on it, he made his way out of the basin and eventually past the decaying pile of logs which marked the cabin where his life had begun.

That may have been where I was born, he thought, but right now I'm just starting to live.

He stopped long enough to dig the pistol out of the roll tied behind the cantle of his saddle and buckle it around his hips. He had not dared wear it in front of Jim and Mary because it would have made him feel foolish then. Now it made him feel wonderful.

Chapter 4

ROSCOE FOUND his first job in southern Colorado with an outfit that was run by a man who had worked with his father. The boy was put to work taking care of the saddle horses. Since the ranch was a fairly old and well-established one, most of the pastures were fenced and the corrals were well laid out.

It was Roscoe's job to bring the horses in to the corrals in the morning and after the men had picked their mounts to take the remuda out to graze on the open range. If the work grew heavy, the crew would want to change horses at noon, but ordinarily Roscoe simply stayed with the herd through the day and brought them into a pasture at night where he could find them in the morning.

It was pleasant work for the most part. Accustomed to solitude, he spent the long sunny days lolling in the saddle or napping in the scant shade his horse cast on some grassy rise. In the evening he would listen with fascination to the men's conversation and fall asleep to dream of stampedes, bucking horses, and wild trips to town.

It was the cook's job to wake him every morning because he and the cook had to get a head start on the rest of the crew. It seemed to Roscoe that he could never get enough sleep. In the cold, black morning he would be shaken awake to dress and stumble to the corrals where his wrangle horse was kept. He saddled and rode out to find the remuda and start them in. Usually the horses would turn toward home and gather speed until they galloped into the corrals, squealing and shying kicks at one another.

There were over a dozen men on the crew, and because his work kept him apart from them so much Roscoe was a long time getting to know them. Most of the men were Texans who talked in a soft-spoken drawl which the boy found pleasant. He was quick to perceive their varying attitudes toward him and was not long in finding out that a kid on a cow outfit was looked upon in many different ways.

Some of the men seemed to consider him a liability, in his ineptitude apt to make extra work for them, some ignored him completely, while others made him the butt of their jokes. But there were a few who remembered their own frightened adolescence and went out of their way to befriend him.

Fortunately for Roscoe the straw boss of the crew, Mark Robbins, exhibited a friendly tolerance toward him. Robbins, a small, fine-boned man with a sandy moustache which drooped incongruously above smiling lips, never allowed his liking for the boy to jeopardize Roscoe's relationship with the rest of the crew. He did not make a pet out of him because this would have surely caused the rest of the men to despise Roscoe and waste no opportunity to "job" him, as they would have put it. Robbins never interfered with the elaborate practical jokes the men played on the boy, or stood between him and the wrath some of his mistakes provoked in the older hands.

But he did talk quietly with the boy at night in the bunkhouse and he did his best to teach him what he could about the outfit and the work. With a polite regard for Roscoe, the foreman took pains to present his suggestions indirectly, almost as if they were hypothetical cases.

"You know," Mark would say, "if a man studies these horses a little, pretty quick he'll get to where he can tell 'em apart in the dark."

Or, "Some of these old-timers get pretty ringy but they don't mean anything by it. It's just that they had a hard way to go making a hand and they want to show there's more to this work than just eat, sleep, and ride a pony."

It seemed to Roscoe that some of the older men devoted much of their time to making life miserable for him. If a single horse managed to hide in the predawn darkness when the boy gathered the herd, one of the men was sure to call for that horse. If two or three horses eluded him they would be missed and mentioned deliberately. The horse herd was held in a corner of the big corral by the men on foot. Mark Robbins and Ben Fluke roped the ponies as the cowboys named the mount they had chosen for the morning. Each of the men had eight to ten horses in his individual "string" and tried to share the work equally among them.

With over a hundred horses milling in the semidark, the ropers exhibited uncanny skill in spotting the animals called for and then snaring them with graceful backhand or overhand tosses. Roscoe stood back to watch the horses caught. To him this roping was a supreme art, and he studied the techniques avidly. Also it was the tensest moment of his day because during the first few months he was never sure that all the horses were in the corral, and he waited breathlessly to see whether or not all the horses called for had been caught.

All too often during the early days of his job as wrangler Mark or Ben would turn away from the herd to the last cowboy, saying, "Can't seem to spot that Chico horse. How about your Big Red, he's here?" If the hand who had called for the missing horse was one of the better sort, he would accept the alternate mount without a word, but if he was not he would curse "that blind bastard of a kid" and make a great show of searching the herd before he settled for a second choice. At such times Roscoe would hang back in the darkness, his face burning with a mixture of anger and shame.

Gradually he became better at the job. He learned to know the horses individually and knew which of them were inclined to quit the bunch and hide. It became a contest between him and the herd. The horses tested him every chance they got, and some of the older ponies seemed to enjoy the game. They would drift gradually off to one side and then stand perfectly still behind a cedar or beside a rock hoping to be overlooked.

Some mornings deviltry and good spirits seemed to infect the whole herd and they would split up, running in every direction but the right one as if they were a band of mustangs unaccustomed to the sight of a rider. Roscoe soon learned that if he simply sat back and let them snort and scamper they would soon tire of the game and head for the home corral.

Each morning when the cook shook him awake an hour before the rest of the crew he had to force himself out of the warm bed. The cook would go off to stoke up his fire, and Roscoe would stumble gummy-eyed to the corrals where one of his horses waited.

It seemed unfair. He could really use more sleep. Some of the older men seemed unable to sleep, and he could hear them coughing or turning restlessly as he fumbled with his pants and boots. Often one or two of them would be smoking, and he could see the red tips of their cigarettes glow and arch in the darkness. They couldn't sleep, why didn't they go out and bring in the horses?

Once Roscoe came awake when he felt his foot being pulled and saw a figure at the foot of his bunk. He grunted and the shadowy form disappeared. The cook rarely said anything; he simply shook him and left. Roscoe drew his union-suited legs out of the blankets and struggled into the rest of his clothes. He was really half asleep and functioning through habit.

At the door of the bunkhouse he sensed that it seemed darker than usual, but he made his way to the corral, caught his horse and saddled. Out in the pasture he saw that the horses were bunched not far from the gate for some strange reason, and it took him only a matter of fifteen or twenty minutes to swing around the fringes of the herd and start them toward the corral. The herd moved along sluggishly, and by the time he had them behind the gate he sensed that something was out of order.

Glancing up toward the cookhouse he saw that it was dark. It should be bright with lamps and "the biscuit shooter" should be clashing stove lids as he worked. The lamps had not been lit in the bunkhouse yet, either. At first he entertained several reasons for the unusual situation, but they were not reassuring. Then he became alarmed and made his way up the slope to the bunkhouse.

Inside a few discordant snores greeted him, and he made his way carefully to the cook's bunk. There he was, sound asleep, his old gray face relaxed, showing only the creases left by his perpetual expression of discontent and his lips collapsed against his toothless gums. Hanging from a nail beside his bunk was the big, thick, dollar watch which, as far as Roscoe knew, was the only clock in the camp. He carried the watch to the window and canted it toward the moonlight. The heavy arrow-shaped hands indicated ten-thirty. Roscoe did not need to put the watch to his ear; he could hear it ticking. Ten-thirty. That meant that he had only been in bed a little over an hour.

He went outside and one glance at the sky showed him that the cook's watch was close to being right.

Wide-awake now, he walked slowly back to the corrals. He opened the gate and let the horses trot back out to the pasture, and after unsaddling his wrangle horse he sat on the anvil beside the saddle room and thought things over. His first reaction was anger. Someone woke him up as a joke, knowing that he would think that it was morning. Who was likely to pull such a stunt? He tried to recall the figure he had mistaken for the cook, but knew that that was no use. Then he began to wonder whether or not he had really felt his foot being pulled. Perhaps one of the men had gotten up to go out and take a leak and simply brushed against his bunk in passing. If this was the case, he would feel pretty foolish revealing what he had done. He decided to keep quiet about the affair and see what developed.

Still puzzled, he went up to the bunkhouse and quietly got back into bed. Roscoe gave the matter a good deal of thought all through the following day, but came to no conclusions. That evening at the supper table the men concentrated on their food as usual, and there was very little conversation until Whitey Burns helped himself to his second plateful and said:

"I got to cut out loading up so heavy at night. Gives me bad dreams. Can't just remember what it was all about, but last night I had nightmares something fierce. Stompedes and runaway horses all over the place."

"It ain't food what does it, Whitey," old Mat Matthews said through a mouthful of meat, "s'bad conscience."

"Dunno," Whitey said, "I ain't had the chance lately to do enough sinning as would bother a man's sleep. This was a real hell-roarer, too. Woke up all asweat pulling at my soogans. Seems like I had spread my bed right where a herd of mustangs was headed at a dead run. Scared me so I thought I could still hear 'em when I came to."

Whitey shook his head and went back to his second helping. Roscoe did not look up from his plate. He felt that something was going to happen, but he was not sure and did not want to give himself away.

"Funny," Slim Harrison said, "now you mention it. I dreamt something about a stompede last night, too. All I can recollect is the noise they made a'running."

Roscoe was almost sure now. He waited, and the subject went up and down the table. It seemed that almost every man on the crew had dreamed of stampedes or runaways the night before. They thought back to the meal they had eaten that night. Nothing unusual there. They debated the causes of bad dreams and speculated about their meaning. Old Mat held out his theory that it was all due to guilty conscience. It seemed to Roscoe that everything was a little too pat, the way they backed each other up and finally turned the spotlight his way.

"Ask young Roscoe," Whitey said. "He's probably got the cleanest conscience here. It's my bet he slept sound. How about it, son?"

Roscoe felt the men staring at him, and he looked up. He tried to detect a smile that would give away their joke, but the faces he could see were earnest. Roscoe heard his own voice, almost as if it were someone else's, say, "Some sonofabitch woke me up."

He blushed furiously and looked down at his plate as the men around the table burst out with roars of laughter. They laughed, choked, coughed, and slapped their thighs. Despite his anger Roscoe began to grin. The men were laughing at him the way that they laughed at themselves or one another.

This was a turning point. It marked the beginning of a new status which he moved into eagerly, so eagerly that he stumbled a time or two. At least he was being noticed by the older men, recognized as a person even though he was not yet accepted as a man.

The recognition flattered him. Through the long summer days he indulged in fantasies testing and shaping his new identity. He rehearsed speeches in which he explained the ways of cow and horse work to an uninitiated boy who followed his every phrase and gesture with admiring eyes.

The first few times that he was allowed to go to town

with the crew were exciting and disappointing at the same time. The boy enjoyed having money to spend and being where he could spend it, but the men would not take him along on their ritual tour of bars and brothels. Roscoe hung around the saddle shop buying gear he needed and some that he did not need simply because of the novelty of having money and spending it. He drank pop until he bloated and never missed a chance to name the outfit he rode for so that he would not be mistaken for a kid.

When the cattle were shipped that fall, Roscoe was told that there would be a job for him over the winter if he wanted to stay. He accepted, and when the bulk of the crew who were leaving to look for work in the south gathered their gear, Roscoe and the three other hands who were staying on went with them to town for a last fling together.

Roscoe was not sure of his emotions. He was glad that he had been asked to stay but sorry that he was not a full-fledged hand who could drift on, confident that he could find another job. During the farewells, Roscoe was included in several rounds of drinks. By swallowing quickly he found that he could get the whiskey down, and when the rounds came too quickly for him he managed to pour his shot into a spittoon when he was not observed. This went on for some time, and then Roscoe found himself on the depot platform with the three others who were to stay over the winter.

The rest of the men were gone, and Roscoe felt very strange. His face was hot and flushed, and there was a roaring in his ears. He seemed detached, remote, and none of the conversation around him made sense. He heard phrases and bits of sentences, a word here and there, so he smiled and nodded when he thought he should and steadied himself against a pole.

Then he found himself in the café seated at a table with the others. They were talking and laughing and chewing with their mouths open. Roscoe smiled and hacked desperately at his steak. He chewed the meat for a long time before swallowing, but when the first bite stayed down he bolted the rest of the meal: potatoes and string beans. The coffee helped, and he actually tasted the pie.

Feeling better, he walked with the three men the length of the town's single street and back. They played several games of pool and Roscoe now felt so well that when they suggested another drink he agreed to a glass of beer. There was more pool, and then they were walking again and Roscoe followed hazily along up the alley onto a porch, into a dimly lit room crowded with furniture.

For a moment Roscoe could not remember the name of the cowboy sitting next to him even though he had worked with him all summer. The man's face was blurred as he turned to say something to Rosoe. Again the roaring and the feeling of heat. Roscoe nodded and smiled and swallowed.

Then there was a confusion of girls. Smells of perfume, the rustle of skirts, laughter, soft white arms, a girl on his lap with a powdered face and bright red lips. The face was fuzzy but the lips were sharply outlined, and Roscoe noticed one front tooth was broken off at an angle. More laughter and movement, and the cowhand on the couch beside him poked him in the ribs. They were getting up, and the girl in Roscoe's lap rose and took his hand, leading him. Up some stairs, down a narrow hall and into a small room where a smoky lamp revealed a single chair and a large brass-posted bed.

He had trouble taking off his boots and was embarrassed in his underwear, but he hurried trembling into the wrinkled bed, aching to accomplish something which he was not sure he knew how to do. The girl, plump, soft, blonde, reached for the lamp exposing rosy-nippled breasts which Roscoe stared at hungrily. In the dark he smelled the kerosene lamp which had just been blown out and plunged his face against the soft round breasts and tasted them and smelled the sweet-sharp unfamiliar body odor, and then he knew that he was going to be sick.

He fought his way out of the covers and was almost free when the contents of his stomach surged up his throat and into his mouth, and he clamped his teeth shut but the hot, bitter, lumpy vomit spewed out on the bed, the blonde, and himself. She screamed and swore, and he struggled to the door, gagging and splattering his dinner all the way.

As he jerked the door open the soft light in the hall seemed brilliant and he paused, wondering which way he should go, when another spasm wrung his stomach and brought up another stream that burned his throat and nose and splashed on the bare floor. The blonde was cursing and pushing him from behind, and doors were opening up and down the hall. A man laughed raucously, and Roscoe stood in the hall as the door slammed behind him, looking down at the puddle at his feet and a green string bean plastered in the downy hair on his belly.

PART

2

<I met Buck Hastings when I was eighteen. By then I figured I'd made a hand and was done with being the kid on the crew. Buck was running the VB for the Bartons up north of Flagstaff. I met him a bar across from the railroad depot. To hear him tell it the VB was just about all of northern Arizona. He was a lot of ways like my father and I took to him. When I asked him for a job he said, "Well, if you can ride young horses and handle cattle there's work for you on the VB because that's two things we've got lots of."

I had a lot to learn about cattle, and the old VB was the place to learn it. They had 'em. I let on to Buck that I really knew my way around, but it didn't take him long to peg me. I got along fine the first few days around the corrals snapping out the string Buck handed me. Some of those ponies cut pretty fancy didoes, but I just ate that up. Then one day he sent me out to hunt up the tail end of some cows that had been left up on fall pasture.

I scouted the country all day and came home with just a handful. Buck never said a word. Next morning he puts me to digging out a spring and sends an old hand up to the same country. The old fart came in that night with a big slug of cows. I sulled around two, three days.

Now, you take old Buck Hastings. When you rode with him you had to be a good man. If you weren't you couldn't keep up. Like that time when we were roping those old mossy-horned steers out of the brush. I was just a kid. I was riding a crackerjack steel dust that made working a pleasure and Buck, he was on a little grulla that wouldn't weigh over eight-fifty. Buck put his twine on a big line-back steer and got jerked down. The rest

51

of us, I forget who all else was there, we jumped right in and got ropes on that steer, but Buck was pinned down under his pony and it took some doing to get him loose. He was under that horse for quite a while. When we got him out he mounted up and spooled his rope and said, "Turn that son of a bitch up."

We let the steer up and Buck, he lit out after it. He dabbed his rope onto the horns, tossed his slack onto the far side, and rode away. He jerked that steer about ten feet straight up in the air and flipped it over. It hit the ground so hard it bounced twice. Buck, he bailed off and gimped over to the steer and had him tied before we got there. Right about then old Buck folded up like a blanket, and we came to find out that his right leg was busted in two places from that horse falling on him.

He was quite a boy, old Buck. In his day he was a real one. A regular curly wolf, and I rode right with him. Like the time we were breaking those colts together and Buck, he said he had a thirst and we ought to go to town. By then I'd learned to drink a little. I don't remember what all we did, but it was plenty. Seemed like every time I'd just about be getting over one trip to town old Buck would come up with another reason for going in and getting all bent out of shape again. We put a lot of mileage on those colts.

One time we quit drinking. Three whole days we never had a drop. We had gave it up. Buck commenced to get cranky and started telling me I needed a haircut and saying how we sure ought to start gentling that light team for the boss, and the next thing I knew we had those two bronco colts hitched to the buckboard. They made a couple of five-mile circles out on the flat before we got them pointed toward town. That was quite a ride.

We stabled the broncs and went right to the barbershop, but somehow we got drunk. I don't remember just how, but there we were with half a dozen guys helping us hitch that team. We had quite a run out from town, and they seemed to be settling down when we came to a pretty rough grade. Old Buck, he had the lines, and he said, "I'm going to scare you, Roscoe." "No," I said. "You can do

a lot of things, Buck Hastings, but that ain't one of them."
So Buck sent that team down the mountain hell for leather.
I hung on and rattled. When they had run themselves
out we let them walk a ways, and when I knew we were
close to a bad stretch along the river I took the lines
and, "Buck," I says, "you want to sit well back in your
rigging 'cause I'm going to make you dirty your pants."
"No," he said, "I don't scare any better than you do."
He didn't, either.

Buck was about the first married cowhand I ever knew,
but then he wasn't just a hand, he bossed the outfit. His
wife was part Indian. She was quite a gal. Cooked for us
there at the home ranch, schooled those two kids, nursed
our hurts. It's tough on a woman wintering out in that
kind of country, but she didn't want to be anywhere Buck
wasn't. She did a good job raising those kids. Don't
know where the girl got to. Off married some place.
'Course you know the boy, Jack Hastings, ramrodding the
same spread, the VB up north of Flag. They don't make
them any better than Jack. He'll never be the hand his
old man was, but that's not his fault. He's probably a
damn' sight smarter than old Buck. Lots of folks who
never knew Buck away back like I did will likely tell you
he was a no-good bum.

Well, toward the last maybe that's what he was. The
last time I saw him there wasn't much of the old Buck
left, he was just another rummy. But in his day he was
the best working foreman I ever rode for. That VB is a
tough outfit to run right, but Buck worked at it like it
was his own and took things as they came and did a good
job. When he thought they were overstocked he went in
and told John Barton, and the boss always backed Buck
up. They trusted him, and he did a good job for them. I
never asked John Senior, but John Junior told me once
that they would have financed him if he had tried to start
out on his own.

I never could figure out why Buck didn't take a whirl
at ranching for himself. Maybe he knew something about
himself that the rest of us didn't. His boy Jack tells me
that he did a lot of planning and plotting about the day

when they would have their own place. I guess he just kept adreaming about it and then it was too late. I guess it got to where it took more and more booze to even dream, and once he knew his time had run out he just jumped clean into the jug and pulled the cork in after him. Jack tells me that when they found him froze stiffer than a poker in a snowbank west of town he had on working clothes. Chaps, spurs, and all. He hadn't been horseback for years, but he was all got up like he was ready for a big drive.

Folks may tell you Buck Hastings died a bum, and for what they know of him they may be right, but I can tell you it wasn't always so. He was good to me when I was a kid and later, too. As long as he was running the VB I knew I had a job if I wanted it. He was tough but he wasn't mean. He never asked a man to do anything that he wouldn't do himself. I've seen him let the chore boy go out on an easy riding job while Buck chopped wood. I've seen him take a snuffy bronc that some younger hand turned down as too rough and just punish himself working that horse. When he got older that got harder for him to do, but he did it just the same.

He was all tore up inside from the beatings he'd taken on rough horses, but just as quick as a man would start shying off from working a horse in his string because it was too snuffy for him, Buck would trade him out of the horse and take to riding it himself. I've seen him top one off in the morning and then get down and lose his breakfast right there in the corral.

I said he wasn't mean, but I'm a liar. Sometimes he got meaner than cat shit when he got drunk. He'd sit there soaking up enough whiskey to kill a horse and get quieter and quieter and the lines around that crooked old broken nose of his would kind of sag and he'd take hold of the bar with both hands and look straight ahead and say real slow, "Roscoe, I don't want no trouble with nobody," and you knew that pretty quick war was going to break out. It might have been he saw somebody he didn't like come in or it might have just been a stranger. Tourists, and dudes, riled him. Somebody wearing cow-

boy clothes that wasn't a working hand was the worst.
Most of the time if you went about it right you could josh
him out of fighting, but sometimes you were wasting your
breath.

The only time you could count on him behaving when
he was in town was when he had the kids along. He had
ideas about raising those kids. The boy, Jack, was a salty
little tyke right from the first. His mom did the best she
could with him, teaching him his lessons and all, but he
never knew any other kids except his sister. He was
always around us hands, and he acted and talked just like
one of us when he was only belt high. His cussing never
bothered Buck unless he was around his mother, and of
course none of us ever cussed in front of her either.

One time we brought little Jack in for something, and
the three of us went to the café for dinner. They had the
dishes wrote out on a slate blackboard on the wall, and
everybody sat at one long table and they brought you
what they had. This old gal that took care of us kept
making a fuss over little Jack. You know how women are
with a kid. She pestered him with all sorts of fool kid
questions and he just clammed up and got red in the
face. She wanted to know how he liked this or that and
what he did out on the ranch. He never said boo. Buck
and me could see he was getting hot, so we went to job-
bing him some. Asked him who his girl friend was and
how he'd managed to get her so sold on him and all. Jack,
he just steamed.

When she brought the kid some ice cream she told him
she bet he didn't get treats like that out on the VB. She
told him he ought to move to town where he could get
food like that all the time. Jack was getting redder and
redder, and me and Buck was winking at each other. "How
do you like the ice cream?" she asked him, and "What
do you get to eat at the ranch?" Little old Jack turned
and looked her right in the eye, mind now he was only
five or six, he looked square at her and said loud as he
could, "Bulls' balls, lady!" She like to fell over.

Buck and me laughed, but Buck spoke to him later
about talking that way. Maybe there was a lot wrong with

the way Buck brought that boy up, but looking at the way Jack turned out I'd say it was a pretty fair country job. Jack is a good man, a man you can count on, and if it hadn't of been for him I'd never of gone back to the VB. You don't find many like him any more.

Wouldn't it be something if you could get together a crew like me and Buck and a half a dozen other old boys when we were in our prime and take them out there to the ranch just for a little bit to show how it should be done? Men you could count on? Like one time when I first worked with him Buck had a crew he'd hand-picked. Good men, every one of them. When you went to rope something you didn't need to worry about whether or not the fellow with you would be able to back you up. He had to be able or he wouldn't be there.

I remember one morning when we were out on a big gather. A dozen of us saddling up in that half light. No corrals to work the horses in; we had to saddle and mount in the open and most all those old range horses would naturally buck before they settled down to a day's work. That day I called for a big hammerheaded dun in my string because we were set for a big circle and he needed the work. I remember I led him out a ways from the wagons 'cause the cook got ringy when we bucked into camp. This old pony was snorting and blowing and just looking for something to spook at, and I rolled a smoke to let him simmer down.

I watched the others catching their horses. I like to watch men do work they're good at. The easy way they'd roll out those big loops and snag a bronc every time. Two men roping and the rest holding lass ropes together around the herd. I finished my smoke and it was light and I saddled up. The old dun threw a knot in his backbone that damn near cocked the rig up on end. I just took up on the back latigo and told him to go ahead and throw all the wall-eyed fits he was a mind to because I was just the boy to teach him some manners. He didn't scare me even a little because I figured I could ride him till he starved to death. I was that cocky.

I took hold of the headstall and stepped in the stirrup

as easy as I could. When I went up onto him I dragged his ugly head around to me so I had his chin right against my knee. I left him no room to mess around in while I shoved my feet deep in the stirrups and got well set in the saddle. When I figured I was ready I turned loose of his head and away we went. That kak of mine came up like a skyrocket. The dun had his head buried back between his front legs and his back bowed like a cat.

He hit the ground with all four feet together, but I was looking for him and gave some when he landed. The next jump he seemed like he went straight up and flung his front and hindquarters in opposite directions so as to send a jolt down his backbone right under the saddle. But hell, I'd been there before. I set easy and balanced and gripped and stayed one jump ahead of him all the time. We worked over toward where the others were busy saddling up, and I took it funny the way they scattered. Confident as all hell and wanting to show off, I reached a spur up and drove it into that old pony away up in his neck. One minute I was riding fine, taking everything that bronc could muster, and the next thing I knew I couldn't find my saddle.

When I hit the ground I hit terrible hard, and I flung my arms over my head when I saw a hoof coming back at me, and just then my surprise at getting unloaded turned into worse than just a scare because I realized my spur was caught under the cinch and I was being dragged. It seemed like a long time before I managed to twist and use my free foot to kick the other spur loose. I kind of had the wind knocked out of me but I wasn't hurt. I got up in a hurry. Not for any good reason but just because it was embarrassing and sort of unnatural to be laying there on the ground.

Just one quick look and I could see that as busy as everybody had been, they were all in action just that quick. Three of the boys had their ropes down with loops built ready to catch that bronc, two had mounted and charged around the herd to head him off, and Buck, who had been standing by the wagon talking to the cook, Buck was just lowering his gun as I got up. That dun horse was jerked up short by two ropes less than fifty yards from where he started. You can bet there wasn't any of them standing around saying, "Oh, my God, look at that!" And there wasn't any damn fools chasing behind that horse making it run away, either.

It made a man feel good to know he belonged to a crew like that. That kind is hard to come by nowadays, though, and knowing it takes a lot of pride out of the work.>

Chapter 5

ROSCOE WAS WORKING in New Mexico. He and a youngster had just come in from a long ride, moving cattle from one water hole that was drying up to another which could carry them. They were leaning against the rough corral fence smoking and studying the skyline of broken rimrock. The horizon was jagged and uneven against the washed-out blue of the sky. Off to the south an abrupt point of rock jutted up.

"That's Stetson Butte, huh, Roscoe?" the kid said, squinting against the smoke from an unaccustomed cigarette.

"That there? Yeah," Roscoe said.

"I'll bet there's mountain lions up there."

"I guess," Roscoe said.

"Let's go lion hunting, Roscoe."

"I ain't lost any lions."

They smoked and the horses in the corral dropped their heads in the heat. A buzzard floated out across the high desert, and the kid sighted on him with one forefinger and flipped his thumb down.

"Bang," he said.

Roscoe watched the buzzard, knowing that the big bird was heading toward a dead cow that lay near the road coming to camp. The boss had said to skin the carcass to salvage the hide, but that was no job for a top hand. Besides, it was coming on toward summer and he was restless. Up in Wyoming the meadows were greening up and the ponies in the cavvy would be shedding off.

"Damn," the kid said, "I got the heartburn from that crap they fed us last night, enough to gag a maggot."

"Stick around," Roscoe said. "You'll learn to digest

anything you can swallow and a whole helluva lot you can't chew."

"How do they feed here?" the kid asked. "I mean set beside other outfits you've ridden for."

"Average," Roscoe said, "just average."

"Back home they feed the harvest gangs a lot better. They get fried chicken, ham, pies, all kinds of good stuff."

"Yeah," Roscoe said. The buzzard was spiraling gently down to where he knew the dead cow lay. It was just too damn hot.

"Oh," Roscoe said, "they feed pretty fair here. They keep that jam and ketchup on the table all the time, and you don't get that a lot of places. They're free with the beef. Some outfits they just pass the beans all the time."

"I like beans," the kid said.

"That's good," Roscoe answered, "if you aim to be a hard-riding, double-tough, hell-raising cowhand you'll likely process a good number of them."

"How do they feed up north?"

"Up north?" Roscoe said, thinking of the green meadows and tumbling streams. "Oh, about the same. Some better I guess, with all the cold weather."

"You ever work in Montana, Roscoe?"

"Montana? Sure."

"What's it like?"

He might even go to Montana. See the old place. Jim and Mary.

"Why, it's like nine months of winter and three that's damn late fall," he said aloud.

"Cold, huh?"

"Cold and windy," Roscoe said. "There's nothing between Montana and the North Pole but a three-wire fence and that don't turn much wind."

A high-backed buggy came up the road below them, pulling a swirling column of red dust behind it.

"Here comes the boss back from town," Roscoe said.

The buggy, drawn by a team of buckskin range horses, drew up beside them and a big florid man in blue serge stepped out. Roscoe could see that he was angry. Now what? Roscoe thought. His face looks mad as a shovel full of hot coals.

"Banks," the big man said, "I told you two days ago to skin out that dead cow down by the salt lick."

"Yeah," Roscoe said.

"Well? Why haven't you done it?"

"I hired on to ride for you, Mr. Ballard, not skin out old dead cows that's been lying around in the sun ripening."

"Just what do you mean?" Ballard almost shouted. He was a head taller than Roscoe and now he seemed to swell with rage.

"I mean what I said," Roscoe said evenly. "I mean just what I said. That's what I mean."

"Well," Ballard said, "on this ranch you do what you're told. The cow may be dead, but the hide's worth something, and when you ride for me you skin 'em when you're told."

"I reckon I'm not riding for you then," Roscoe said.

"You're damn right. Spool your bed and head for the highway."

Ballard turned to the boy.

"Peel the hide off that cow," he said and then went toward the house in his peculiar loping gait.

Roscoe watched him go and felt strangely elated.

"Big sonofabitch," he muttered.

"Jeeze, Roscoe," the kid said, "now you went and got yourself canned."

"I made a living a long time before I came here," Roscoe said, "and I'll likely go right on after I leave."

"Well," the kid said, "I better start knocking the back off that old cow. Phew! I can smell her just thinking about it."

"Take a team down and jerk the side off," Roscoe said. "It'll save you having to get down and handle her."

"How do you mean?"

"Start peeling the hide back off the neck and tie it to a chain. Then split her down the belly and legs. Tie her head to something handy like a juniper and then hitch your team to that chain you tied to the hide in front. If you've got her started and split right, all you have to do is drive your team away."

"The hide'll come right off?"

"Slicker than butter."

"That's pretty neat," the kid said. "Where'd you learn about that?"

"Hell," said Roscoe, "when I was a kid we used to skin out all the old cows that died."

"Why wouldn't you skin out this one?"

Roscoe looked at the kid for a moment, glanced toward the house, and then spat very deliberately in the red dust at his feet.

"There's just a lot of things I wouldn't do for that big sonofabitch," he said and turned toward the bunkhouse.

Roscoe went north, but he got no farther than Colorado. There in a little cowtown bar he met a man named Tad Burnham, a skinny scarecrow of a man with a dolorous pockmarked face, who struck up a conversation with Roscoe and after a few drinks said:

"Banks, eh? Wouldn't be related to Hal Banks that was killed in Wyoming in '92, would you? You look like him."

"Yes," Roscoe said. "He was my father."

"The hell! Never knew he had a kid."

Roscoe waited nervously, but Burnham changed the subject and talked at length about his experiences in the Spanish-American War. Finally it became more than Roscoe could bear.

"Did you know my father?" he asked.

Burnham sipped at his glass of whiskey.

"In a way," he said. "I was there when they killed him. You knew about that?"

"Just that they shot him figuring he was somebody else, a cow thief."

The ugly face lifted, and Roscoe looked into Burnham's murky eyes.

"There was no mistake," Burnham said evenly. "They knew just what they were doing. The bastards!"

Roscoe flushed and suddenly wished he had never seen

this man, that he was somewhere else, anywhere. Burnham looked away, toward the back bar where the bottles stood in a row. As Roscoe looked at his profile the thin lips began to move and the whining voice told the story that Roscoe dreaded to hear. He stood fascinated, unconsciously twisting the heavy shotglass on the bar.

It had been early in the spring, Burnham said, of '92. He was sixteen and was working for an old trapper named Dan Law. They had been on their way in to the town of Buffalo when night fell, and since it looked as though it would snow before morning they decided to spend the night in an abandoned homestead that the old man knew about.

When they reached the cabin they found that two cowboys whom Dan knew were established there for the winter. They welcomed the company and helped put the horses in the ramshackle barn. Old Dan brought in his fiddle, and after supper he played for them and they talked late that night.

"I was just a punk kid," Burnham said, "and I sat pretty well back listening to them talk. Hal Banks and Dick Harlow, they were. Old Dan knew them from a long time back. They had a herd in the breaks below the house, and they were figuring on some kind of a government contract. I didn't just get the straight of it. They talked a lot about the way things were going, what with rustling and all, and they seemed to think trouble was brewing."

Burnham shook his head. If he had known, he said, he would have been long gone out of there. But they finally went to bed. In the morning Dan had gone out with a bucket to the creek for water. When he did not come back for some time, Tad went to look for him. As he rounded the corner of the barn he walked into the muzzle of a Winchester and was hustled down the creek into a clump of willows where he found Dan held captive by several heavily armed men. They were questioned. Suddenly they heard a shot, and after a brief pause a volley rattled off the walls of the canyon.

"A man came running down to where we were,"

Burnham said, " 'Dick Harlow stepped out and we got him but Banks dragged him inside,' this guy said. Old Dan started cussing and they clubbed him. Then they went up toward the cabin. Dan said he knew one of the men. Called him Hank Henry. There was a lot of shooting. It started to snow and I was cold, scared, and pure miserable. A long time later they set fire to the cabin. We could smell the smoke. I peeked out through the branches.

"Somebody yelled, 'There he goes yonder,' and I saw Banks coming toward the creek, running, kind of bent over. He had a rifle in his left hand a six-gun in the other. He snapped a couple of shots with the pistol while he was running, and they opened up. You could see the dust raise off his jacket where the bullets hit him. He sort of jerked and kept coming, and little puffs of dust blew up off his coat and he went down and they kept on shooting."

Roscoe listened and saw the whole thing, and he flinched at the picture of each slug tearing its way through the body of this man who had been his father.

"They came and roughed me and old Dan up some and told us to head south and keep going and to keep our mouths shut if we knew what was good for us. We did like they said and split up a couple of weeks later. I never went back but a fellow told me that Dan Law did. He said they found old Dan up in the Powder River country all shot to hell just a while after I left him down in southern Wyoming. I figured those jaspers meant what they said so I never went back. If you're smart you'll stay away yourself."

Roscoe picked up his drink and gulped it off as if he were trying to break a trance, to rid himself of the image of his father lying in the rocks twitching under the impact of the bullets. If they knew who he was, he reasoned, they must have figured Hal was a thief. People have long memories.

"Well, I got to be getting," Burnham said abruptly. "Stand around here running off at the mouth like a old woman."

He nodded at Roscoe and was gone, but Roscoe did not notice. He was remembering conversations he had heard between Jim and Mary when he was in bed in the loft above them. The questions they asked each other about the cattle Hal had brought. Did they think Hal had been a thief? It seemed to him that they must have. No, he would not go back to Montana. Like Burnham, he would stay well away, but not for Burnham's reasons. Suddenly Roscoe felt lonely.

This loneliness followed him for some time as he worked around the country. It drove him. To keep him company he began to daydream about a girl he had seen at a rodeo in Flagstaff. She had been sitting close to the chutes when Roscoe made a ride that had won him first prize, and she had smiled and applauded when his name had been announced as winner of the event. Roscoe had never forgotten her even though he never spoke to her and did not even know her name.

Gradually, over the years, he had been forced to touch up her picture, as it were, because the actual memory was fading. Eventually she became almost entirely a figment of his imagination. From the length and color of her hair to her personality, he added one detail after another. He called up her image in the dark lonely nights and the long monotonous days.

She rode beside him on a neat pony with easy grace, or sat opposite him by his campfires. He explained himself to her over and over, telling her things that he would never tell anyone else, and she always understood and took his side. When he rode out a big salty bronc she was watching and he was proud. He began to conduct himself according to her point of view and to ask himself whether she might approve of this or that or how he would be able to explain himself to her for doing such and such.

Chapter 6

WHEN HE MET Ruby she was not at all like his imaginary girl friend. Ruby was plain and colorless by comparison. Even shyer than Roscoe, she hid herself from him when Roscoe first went to work for her father breaking colts. She was the eldest of nine children and kept busy with chores while the younger members of the family watched through the corral fence "to see the bronc peeler piled."

Roscoe did not stay at the homestead long. There were only six young horses to be started and he had them going well in short order. Each morning he caught all six colts and tied them along the corral fence. In the course of the day he would handle and ride each of them in turn. At first things were exciting enough, but in a month the work was getting dull and he was ready to move on.

<I hardly ever saw her except at table. She'd be at the stove a lot even then. When her mom would shoo her to eat she'd just stare at her plate and I was just as glad 'cause I was embarrassed, too. Don't know why. Not unless it was because I knew she was a real good girl and I was such a bum.>

Roscoe left when the colts were gentle and assumed that he would probably never see the little ranch or Ruby again, but that winter, working on a large ranch in Texas, he was surprised to find that he kept remembering her face. The thin little face with overly large brown eyes framed by straight dark hair. He found himself talking to her during the shimmering days as he rode the endless fence lines, and one day he realized that she had replaced his imaginary girl.

<I dunno why. She was little and skinny and frail looking and never even said boo to me when I was up there working for her dad.>

In the spring Roscoe started north riding one horse and hazing another with his bedroll tied to it. Although it was well out of his way, he decided to swing by the ranch and see how the colts he had started were doing. This is what he told himself, at any rate. Ruby was returning from the soddy which served as a henhouse when he rode into the yard. She had her apron gathered up in front carrying eggs.

<The other kids hollered and ran out and she just stood there, and I looked right over the kids at her and she smiled right at me and I knew I never came up there to see those colts.>

That evening in a long and uncomfortable conversation he mentioned to Ruby's father, Jacob Brimmel, that he had been thinking for a long time about homesteading a piece of range in New Mexico. The dour old Dutchman sucked at his pipe and heard him out.

It was a good piece of land, Roscoe said, that he found when he was running horses in that part of the country. Not fit for farming, he said, but a fine place for cattle with lots of open range around it. Jacob nodded noncommittally and flexed his stubby fingers as he studied a cracked knuckle. Roscoe talked on about the country and his plans and said that he was on his way over there now to stake his claim. He asked advice, and the dark-haired Jacob answered in monosyllables.

Then in a rush Roscoe blurted out the fact that when he had gotten a start he wanted to come back and make Ruby his wife. Jacob looked up at him quickly through bushy black brows, looked away, and said nothing. Roscoe could feel his heart pounding. The old man raised his head slowly.

"You are a good man, Roscoe," he said. "You say nothing. Go find your claim and when you come back we will talk again. I will say nothing. When you come back will be time enough."

Roscoe left the next morning without seeing Ruby. He was afraid to. He rode west and knew what wise old Jacob meant. Not "when you come back," but "if you come back." Well, he would come back alright. This was one fiddle-footed saddle tramp that was going to settle down and amount to something and show them all that the cream hadn't all been skimmed off, that a little savvy and cow sense and hard work could add up to a good little spread. Nothing a man would get rich on, but a real good one-man operation.

<Turned out to be about the hardest work I ever did in my life. Nothing easy to it. After I filed on the claim I wanted and threw together a sort of a shanty, I hurried right back to get Ruby. I guess her folks had talked it over with her. She hid out when I came and I didn't see her till she came to table that evening. She was all red in the face and I was too, I guess.

After it got dark we took a walk out on the prairie and I tried to talk it over with her. It was a lot harder saying everything when she was there listening than it had been before. But being dark and all I managed to get most of it said. She said she thought it sounded fine and then it got some easier to talk.>

Old Jacob gave them a team, wagon, stove, and milk cow. Ruby and her mother cried together after the wedding. The wind blew all that night and toward morning it began to snow. The bride and groom set out early on what proved to be a long cold trip.

<Funny thing, nowadays I have trouble remembering Ruby's face, just great big brown eyes and straight black hair, but I can still see that team old Jacob gave us. The damnedest mismatched pair of horses anybody ever paired up. Jim and Jill. Jim, he was a big roan gelding. Stood about sixteen-two and the color of dirty dish water. The longest-headed horse I ever did see and big platter feet that toed away out so he looked like he was walking off in all directions. An honest old goat, though. If you hitched him to a mountain he'd start to pulling and keep right at it till you told him to stop. Never got excited, just a good steady horse.

That Jill now, she was a caution. Smaller than Jim but just about as heavy because where he was long and rangy she was chunky and wide. She was shiny black and flighty as hell. That mare had more imagination than any one horse is entitled to. Seems like she spent all her time looking for something to spook at. She'd shy at her shadow. Snort and sidestep and act like she was trying to get around behind Jim. Jim, he'd cock his ears and look to see what all the fuss was about and when all he could see was the shadow he'd just go right on while Jill jigged and switched her tail and blew and tossed her head.

She was a sly one. She had a little bouncing way of going that made her hind end jiggle up and down like she was on parade and if you didn't watch her she'd let old Jim pull the whole load. Jim would stretch his big ugly head out and lean into the collar while Jill jigged along just keeping the traces tight. She looked like she was working like hell, but all she was doing was keeping up, not pulling a thing. If you gave her any kind of a licking she'd blow sky-high and act like she had no idea what it was all about. She'd lunge and dance and raise all kinds of hell and old Jim, he'd go right along. About the time you wished you had never taken the strap to her she'd settle into that phony switch-tail gait and there you'd be with Jim pulling the whole load again.

I had to build a dirt tank to catch runoff water. It was one of the first things I did when we got home. I had traded for a old fresno. You know, one of those scrapers with a bar on the back you could regulate the bite with and tip it over to dump. Well, I took the team and a plow and the fresno and went at it. First I'd plow out what I wanted and then haul the dirt to the bank with the scraper. It was slow work and that damn mare was giving me fits. If we hit a rock she'd lunge ahead before I knew it.

That would just flip the fresno over and about half the time I'd be caught leaning on the handle behind trying to raise the front of the bucket. If I had a good solid grip the bar would fling me clean up into the horses. I'd fall in amongst their feet and the mare would go nuts. Old Jim would snake his head around and stare at me while I untangled myself and Jill would jump up and down like there was a cougar on her back. If I wasn't holding tight when she dumped it the bar would come up and catch me in the ribs and pound the hell out of me. Hardest work I ever did do.

One time I went to pull a stump with the team. I admit it was tough going, but it could be done. Jim, he leaned into it with that kind of a sad, stupid look on his face, but that dingy mare just blew sky-high. I'd had about all I could take out of her so I cut me a stick and massaged her where I thought it would do the most good. Didn't help. When she saw I aimed to beat her to death on the spot, she threw her head over across Jim's neck and sulled. Just balked all together. I got behind and talked to them, and Jim leaned into it but Jill stood there spraddle-legged with her head tossed back and her eyes rolled around so all you could see was whites. I cussed her and whipped her and nothing happened.

I'd seen a roundup cook cure a balky one time, so I took a pigging string and wrapped it tight as I could around the pastern of her front leg. Wrapped it round and around till it was used up and tied it hard and fast and got behind to watch. After a bit the rope cut off the circulation in that leg and she commenced to get uncomfortable. Pretty soon she stamped her foot. It wasn't long before she straightened up and started to paw.

I picked up the lines and clucked at them and she got right down beside Jim and pulled like an honest horse. We got the stump out and I took the string off her leg. Ever after when she'd sull I'd walk up and let her see a little rope and she'd blow and shake her head and get to work.

Three years I worked that mare and never got ahead of her. She would always test me. If it hadn't of been for

Jim I don't think I would of ever gotten anything done. God help me if I'd of had two like her. Only good thing about her was she was a good keeper. In the winter she would stay sleek and fat while Jim got poor as a snake.>

The milk cow Jacob had given them was a brindle of mixed breeding who made a habit of deliberately aborting herself just before her calf was due to be born by jumping back and forth across a ditch until she sloughed off the premature calf. They had a chicken who would come to the kitchen to beg scraps and then lay her daily egg in the woodbox, a shepherd dog who stole newly hatched chicks and tried to mother them, and an owl who persisted in trying to build a nest in the stovepipe.

They were happy when Ruby became pregnant. Happy until the long drought descended upon them, bringing the steady oppressive heat, the withered grass, the dry wind, the shrunken cattle, and the wagons of other homesteaders who moved out in the face of the inevitable destruction.

Each day he rode out with a shovel to try to clear the muddy springs as one by one they dried up and the cattle stamped them into barren pockets. Each night he rode home more discouraged than ever to help Ruby as much as he could.

One evening he came into the kitchen in time to see her at the stove straining a precious quart of muddy water through a folded flour sack into the coffeepot. As the water passed through the cloth it left a heavy deposit of silt and wriggling water lice. Roscoe watched his wife, clumsy in her pregnancy, and knew that he had waited too long. I should have taken her in last week, he told himself, though she's not due for at least a month. When a cow settles like that you know she's near ready.

Ruby straightened slowly and pushed a strand of hair back from her forehead. She looked even smaller now that her swollen belly exaggerated the narrowness of her shoulders and hips. Her light-boned arms hung like sticks beside her frail body.

"Well," she said, "there's morning coffee, anyway."

"How you feeling, Rube?" Roscoe asked.

"I'm fine, outside of being dry."

"You want to try and get over to Cain's?"

"I reckon not," Ruby said wistfully. "I got a while yet. I just hope they don't pull out before the time comes."

The cattle were bawling their never ending complaint against the drought. It was by now a constant sound that they went to sleep hearing and woke up to in the hot dawn. Gaunt and swollen-tongued, the thirsty animals bawled steadily as the red sun dropped into the barren hills. Roscoe and Ruby lay together on their thin mattress and heard without listening, heard when they tried not to, the spiritless moaning of the cows.

"Let's give it up, Rube," Roscoe said. "Let's pull out."

"We can't, Roscoe," she said softly. "It'll rain."

"We've been saying that for a long time," Roscoe said. "We've been saying it just because it always has rained, some time. This time it looks like it just can't."

"It will though."

"Maybe," Roscoe said, "but if it doesn't hurry up it won't do any good. They're better than half dead right now."

"It will," she said, "and the springs will start and the grass will grow and we'll be right here when the others come back."

"Maybeso," Roscoe said without conviction.

He finally fell asleep and dreamed of being caught in a herd of thirst-crazed cattle stampeding toward a river which dried up as they approached and turned from a rushing stream into a widely cracked mud flat. The bawling of the dream cattle became louder and then he was awake listening to his own cows crying for water in the hot night. Roscoe listened in spite of himself and then he slept again.

The cattle were still bawling when Ruby woke him and they kept on as he tried frantically to help her. When the sun rose, full of heat and promising another day just like all the rest, they bawled as he dug the grave. He lifted shovels full of dry dirt from the deep, narrow trench and the cattle drew curiously around, moaning and bawling, but he no longer heard them. He did not even hear his own wrenching sobs.

<Blood. Never saw so much blood in my life. Looked like somebody had butchered a steer right there in the bed. Just wouldn't stop. Packed her with blankets and she lay quiet and said she felt some better, but she was bleeding all the time. Her face got whiter and whiter. Her lips were the same color as her face. Her feet got cold. Damnedest thing. Must of been close to a hundred and she said her feet were cold. I rubbed them for her. She smiled and closed her eyes and I thought she was asleep until her mouth sagged open and she was dead.>

Chapter 7

AFTER RUBY'S DEATH Roscoe rode north, turning his back on droughts, completely through with thoughts of marriage or trying to start on his own in the cow business. As far as he was concerned, Roscoe Banks was "cured." He made up his mind to concentrate simply on being the best cowhand that he could be and to leave the dreams of running their own cattle to the other boys.

<I wasn't too happy with the idea at first. You know how you can get away ahead of yourself dreaming. It's kind of tough to chuck out all the dreams. But I healed up. Oh, there were scars to show for it and they itched now and again. I'd be working for some dummy and he'd say to go do this or that and I'd catch myself thinking about how, if it was my outfit, things would be done different.

Then I got to where I was wagon boss or ramrod and

I'd listen to what the bosses wanted done and I knew what could be done and the best way to go about doing it. I got to where I came to find out that no matter how good a man a boss was or how much he knew about the work there was something about being a boss that made it hard for him to remember just what the work involved, and I'd figure a way to come as close to what he wanted as you could get with what you had to work with.

It's kind of like a man telling you to go fence a three-section field with a five-wire fence and be back in half a hour. Can't be done, but besides that he only gives you enough wire to go around the field once. You have to sit down and figure out what you can get done for him and how soon and then see to it that that's what gets done. The right man in a job like that is worth a lot.

Worked for a fellow one time that was a great hand to pray. Sometimes he'd tell me to get the rest of the boys in the bunkhouse down on their knees and hold a gospel session for whatever he figured he needed right then: either for the snow to stop or the rain to start or the market to rise or the feed to hold out. I didn't hold much with that praying business and neither did the rest of the boys. Oh, we had nothing against it if a man was convinced in that direction, but it was just that none of us was sold on it.

When you have to live as close to the weather as we did, you know it is going to do just what it damn well pleases, praying or no praying, and as far as the market is concerned we figured God Himself didn't even know what made it work, so it wouldn't do any good to ask Him about it.

No. It wasn't so much that we didn't believe in God the way preachers want you to. It was just that . . . well, like when your cows start calving out the same time as they always have year after year, only this time a freak blizzard comes up and the calves freeze to the ground quick as the old cows drop them and no amount of licking or nuzzling will get them up. Or like a drought. Or Ruby. If He's really running this show, like some believe, then He doesn't really give a damn. A man just has to get out in it and do what he can to save what he can, and that's it. Getting down on your knees and begging is kind of humiliating, and it doesn't seem to do much good anyway.

Oh, like I said, I've prayed. You bet. Like the time I had a horse get hung up in some wire the flood brought down a river. We were out in the middle of her and swimming deep and this old pony flounders. I had to bail off and get his leg loose and I lost hold of him. Anyway we both went downstream, and I didn't think I knew how to swim. I started praying and promising and all I did was take on more water so I decided to quit asking for help and start helping myself. I forget how I did it, but I waved my arms and kicked my feet and after a helluva time I got out of there.

You don't pray your way out of a bad spot or a tough job. It's got to be done so you do it whether you like it or not. If you don't do it then you and everybody else knows that you're a phony and you might just as well spool your bed and leave. We had a job of work to do, and doing it we had to know we could count on ourselves and each other. If you were by yourself you'd go at it one way. With somebody else you'd go at it another, but when you did you knew you could count on whoever was with you. I know all I need to about a man if I know he can keep up his end of the stick. How he feels about doing it is his business. Maybe he is scared, but that's his business and none of mine. It's just kids that go around telling each other how they wet their pants. I don't want anybody nosing around in my business and I don't nose around in theirs.

Men and horses are a lot alike when it comes to getting a job done. People that don't know make a lot of fuss over both of them. They try to make a hero out of a man and a damn pet out of a horse. They're both of them just tools, more or less. Take the average cow pony. You know him. You know what he's good at and what he can't do so good. When you go at getting something done you set him at it the way you think he can handle the job. For instance, let's say he's real handy and quick. He can really jump out and score a critter on the short distance, but he plays out and can't hold up for the long run. Well, knowing this you know you'd be wasting your time trying to run something down so you have to figure out a way you can work up close. The other way around, if he's slow starting but real long-winded you use him another way.

There's good horses and bad, just like men, but they've both got to be halfway honest. Nothing wears you out faster than riding a lazy horse, unless it's trying to get work out of a lazy man. If they're honest and you use them right, you can usually get the job done one way or another. If they know what they're doing it makes it a lot easier. It's downright dangerous to try to do something with a green colt or a green hand if you get them in over their head. They can be as honest as the day is long, but if they don't have the savvy they can kill you.>

News of the outbreak of World War I in Europe was two weeks old when it reached Roscoe in an eastern Oregon camp. Homer Smith, a tall, laconic puncher who affected a perpetually sorrowful expression, brought the papers with their heavy headlines when he came to the camp with supplies.

"Only a matter of time afore we're in it," Homer told Roscoe.

"Not you and me, Homer," Roscoe said, "we're too old."

During the weeks that followed, Roscoe went through his long working days trying to decide what the war would mean to him. The younger men talked of nothing else and joked lightheartedly about deadly subjects. In town he heard rumors of huge contracts for horses to be sent abroad.

"They'll buy anything," a stranger told him with an air of confidence. "If they can't ride it or drive it they'll eat it."

With the unnumbered herds of renowned Oregon horses running loose on the high plateaus of bunch grass, Roscoe felt sure that here was a chance to make the war pay off.

He and Homer planned feverishly all that winter, and spring found them headed for the high desert with everything they could borrow invested in running horses, pack animals, and supplies.

The country that they rode through showed signs of being heavily populated by horses and the farther they went the thicker the signs became. The bunch grass dragged at their stirrups as they climbed from one tableland to another. Each night he and Homer hobbled or staked the horses carefully so that they would not run off or be lured away by a wild bunch. When they chose the location for their base camp it was in a long valley crisscrossed by a sparkling stream.

It took them nearly three weeks to build a rough pen and two corrals at the head of the valley. Occasionally during the crisp clear nights they would hear the thunder of a band of wild horses moving down the valley. Once a big gray stallion with cropped ears stood on the shelf above them and watched the two men at work. Homer leaned on his shovel and stared back at the stud.

"I don't much like these old country ponies with their ears froze off," he said, narrowing his eyes against the sun. "A man needs a handle sometimes."

Roscoe drew a sleeve across his face and looked toward the stallion.

"Muley or Longhorn," he said, "where he's going won't matter."

"No," Homer said, "them foreigners don't seem to mind. Not like our army where they all got to be solid colors and the same size."

A week later the gray stallion and fifteen of his band were in the crude corral and that fall, when the first soft flurry of snow warned them out of the high country, the gray, a gelding now, was driven to the railroad pens with the rest of the summer's catch.

Gentle horses were mixed with the wild ones, and each of the mustangs had a short cotton rope tied to a front foot and run back between the hind legs to be tied to its tail. Hobbled this way, they could not run and limped along following the trained lead ponies. Roscoe rode in front of the herd and Homer behind.

<I built up quite a stake, but I piddled it away rodeoing, horse racing and the like. I always figured a man that was scared of spending his money wasn't sure he could make more. I stuck with the notion for a long time. I got older, but I never got much smarter.>

Chapter 8

THERE WERE good jobs and bad ones, good bosses and bad. But there were always good men to ride with like wiry little red-headed Dink Roberts. Roscoe and Dink were already old friends when they found themselves working together on a ranch owned by an Eastern syndicate and bossed by a man named Jack Mosely. Mosely was the wrong man for the job and Dink and Roscoe were complaining about him to one another as they came riding into the corrals one morning when the wind shifted and slapped them in the face with the stench from the pigpen located below the barn. There were only a few pigs in the pen, just enough to keep up with the garbage, but from the smell it seemed that there should have been a large number of them. The pigs were one of Mosely's innovations, and he made a great thing of the pork feeds he put out for the crew.

The cowboys ate the pork and said little to his face, but in private they swore that they would settle for beans three times a day to be rid of the stench. Roscoe and Dink twitched their noses in disgust as the heavy odor seeped into their nostrils, overpowering all other smells.

"Dink," Roscoe said, "if there's anything in this world

that smells half as rank as pigs I sure don't ever want to meet it."

Dink twisted his spare frame in the saddle and looked back at Roscoe as they entered the big corral. He sucked at a lip full of snuff and spat casually.

"How long has it been," he asked, "since you got downwind from your socks and took a good whiff?"

"Hell," Roscoe said, "compared to those stinking pigs my socks are just like a bunch of violets."

"Maybeso," Dink replied, "but last night in the bunkhouse when you set them out to air I went to sleep dreaming I was cutting steaks off a side of spoiled beef."

"Go on, you probably just got your head into your bedroll and spent the night breathing through your drawers."

An old rough-coated Shire workhorse stood tied to the far side of the corral with his head down and one tattered hoof cocked.

"What's the old horse in here for?" Dink asked as they unsaddled.

"Oh," Roscoe said, "I forgot to tell you. Mosely said this morning that he was going to take that roan colt away from you and give you the Shire for your string."

"Yeah, and if you ate regular you know what you'd do."

Roscoe chuckled and swung his saddle up to a peg in the rack room where he hung it by a stirrup.

"Old Mosely's probably crippling around cussing that Figure Four horse for bucking him off this morning," he said.

"Yeah," Dink said, smiling. "I bet you got a new horse in your string."

"Figure Four? Hell, that goat can't pitch hard enough to scatter salt. He don't worry me even a little bit."

They stood in the shade of the doorway and looked out at the corral which shimmered with heat. Their horses rolled enthusiastically and then trotted past the old Shire, who was tied to the fence, and galloped out to the pasture. Dink took a can of snuff out of his shirt pocket and thumped the bottom of the can deliberately a few times before taking out a wad of the black tobacco between his thumb and forefinger and stuffing it into the pouch of his lower lip. He spat into the corral dust.

Luke Stringer, the cook, came down the slope from the kitchen carrying a thirty-thirty. He was a little bandy-legged man with lines drawing down his mouth. He did not see Roscoe and Dink in the saddle room and went to the old workhorse without glancing their way. They watched as he led the Shire out the corral gate and around toward the pigpens. The flat snapping noise of a shot came shortly after he had disappeared and was followed by the frantic grunts and squeals of the ever hungry pigs. Roscoe rolled a cigarette and watched Luke go back up to the cook shack. Dink sent a stream of spit out the doorway and Roscue struck a match.

"That's what I like about riding for these syndicates," Roscoe said. "When you put your time in year after year, and get to where you can't keep up with the young fellows, they're real good about pensioning you off."

"Yeah," Dink said, "they're real fine that way."

"Funny, when you think about it," Roscoe said, "I've worked on some little outfits where they didn't have half enough pasture and there was always two or three old retired horses turned out on the grass. Just eating and dozing. Taking it easy. But on a big spread like this that's owned by half a dozen people you never see, what happens? The minute they take a notion a horse is past its prime they chicken him or feed him to the pigs."

"Yeah," Dink said, "they call it their 'retirement plan.' "

"But they keep a bunch of spoiled outlaw broncs in the remuda and we have to ride them," Roscoe said. "If they're so worried about their feed that they have to kill off all the old horses, why don't they get rid of half those worthless fit-throwing snakes?"

"Talk to Mosely, Roscoe. After this morning maybe he'll feel like getting rid of some of the spoiled ones."

"He really got spread out, didn't he?"

"He went up the full length of his bridle reins, spread out just like a big old bullfrog."

Dink stepped to the door and spat again.

"You know," he said, "a big horse like that can hurt you more if you stay on him than he will piling you off."

"Yes," Roscoe answered, "but Mosely spends so much time looking for a soft spot to land on he doesn't even try to ride him. When he sees that head go down he damn near jumps off."

"If he'd ride him out a couple of times old Figure Four might get to where a man could talk him out of bucking," Dink said. "He's going to get you to do the riding."

"That horse isn't hard to ride," Roscoe said. "If you figure on going off you sure as hell will. If he would just stay ahead of him and spur hard he could get the job done. Just don't weaken and you can whip that kind."

"Take a deep seat and a long rein, huh, Roscoe?"

"Yeah."

"Well," Dink said with a grin, "it's good you can handle that kind because I just got a notion you're going to get him in your string."

"I can ride him all right, but I think a man ought to get paid for breaking out the rough string while he's doing cow work too."

"Sure," Dink said.

"I've got just one gentle horse in the seven of mine," Roscoe said, "and Mosley couldn't even ride that one."

"Yeah," Dink said, "I know. They mean that for a compliment, Roscoe, because you're such a good hand. As long as they've got a triple-distilled bronc stomper like you they figure they can get these spoiled horses ridden. I'm sure glad that they haven't taken a notion that I might get the job done on that kind. I think I'll let myself get bucked off a couple of times a month just so they don't start thinking I can ride much."

Dink grinned at Roscoe, showing his yellow snoose-stained teeth.

"Yes sir," Dink went on, "they're complimenting you."

"That's dandy," Roscoe said, "real fine."

"They'll give you a medal maybe."

"Yeah," Roscoe grumbled, "but they better start putting something in the kitty."

"Why don't you trade him your Lucky Strike horse for that Figure Four?"

"Mosely would dirty his pants," Roscoe said. "He gets the shakes when I just call for that horse in the morning when we're roping them out. He gets out of the corral before I get saddled."

"That's a mean little horse."

"Yes," Roscoe said, "and he's never going to change any. That's one *caballo* you can pull a wet saddle blanket off of every day for a year and he'll still want to fight you."

"If it was me," Dink said, "I know what I'd do."

"Yeah?" Roscoe said.

"You know how Mosely's all the time going into town? Well, the next time he does why don't you cut out your whole string and drive them up to Horse Springs and turn them loose. They'd join up with that band of mustangs and go off in the brush. They'd never see them again."

"Hell," Roscoe said, "that kind are just ornery enough to come back."

"Well," Dink said, "we're going to start out with the wagon to brand in a day or so. Why don't you get the kid, the wrangler, to cut out your string and lose them along the way?"

"I'll ride them," Roscoe said. "I'll ride them, but they ought to pay for it."

"Here comes Mosely now," Dink said. "Jump him out about it."

A heavyset man with flushed red complexion limped across the corral toward them. He was frowning under the wide brim of his dirty gray Stetson.

"What's the matter, boss?" Dink said. "You got a gimp in your get-along?"

"Yeah," the foreman said as he stepped into the shade of the little room. "I think that sonofabitch busted my ankle when he piled me this morning. I'm going to town and see the doc about it."

"Get me some Copenhagen," Dink said, "will you?"

"Sure," Mosely said. "Anything you want, Roscoe?"

"I guess not," Roscoe said, "unless you want to bring back a bottle or two."

"You know they don't like whiskey in camp," Mosely answered. "I'd like to have a little myself."

Yes, Roscoe was thinking, and you're going to get a snoot full of it in town.

"Well," Roscoe said aloud, "if they won't let you bring whiskey to the crew how about taking the crew to the whiskey? Let's all go in. I've got a thirst."

"I'm coming right back out tonight," Mosely said. "We've got to get ready to go out branding. We'll all go in when that's done."

Dink stepped to the door again and sent a stream of juice out into the sunlight. Roscoe watched the way the spit rolled in the dust and then stood in little balls like quicksilver. Dirty quicksilver, he was thinking.

"Say, Roscoe," Mosely said, "ride that damn Figure Four horse for a while, will you? Maybe you can iron a few wrinkles out of him and then I'll take him back. I won't be able to work on him much until this ankle's better."

Yes, Roscoe said to himself, you'll take him back. If I once put a leg over that bronc I'll be stuck with him just like I am with all the others. You won't come within a mile of riding him as long as you think he's got a fart left in him.

"Well," Roscoe said, "I guess I could do that. He's a pretty stout horse for a big circle. Be handy to have for the gathers we're going to have to make branding. What do they pay a man for riding rough string here?"

"Well," Mosely said and a worried frown creased his florid face, "I don't really know, but they won't hold still for any kind of a raise for any of you fellows just now. You know what the market is doing. I just wouldn't dare bring it up. Maybe this fall, when we ship the weaners, I could jack them up for more money. I know you deserve it. Nobody can tell me that you boys don't earn . . ."

"When are you leaving for town?" Roscoe interrupted.

"What?" Mosely asked.

"When are you taking off?"

"Why, right away. Why?"

"Let Dink and me get our gear together and we'll ride in with you," Roscoe said.

"But," Mosely started, "I just told you . . ."

"Yeah," Roscoe said, "you told me. Now I'm telling you. I'll get my outfit and ride in with you. So will Dink. You think they've got enough money in the till to pay us off?"

"Pay you off?"

"I guess so. If the outfit is so close to being broke as you make out I guess a man ought to get his money out of them while he can. Maybe things are better up north. Maybe up there they can pay a man for the work he does."

Roscoe pulled his saddle down from its peg and carried it out to the fence. Dink followed suit.

"Now wait," Mosely said quickly "Don't get excited. I'll ask the bookkeeper. I'll see what I can do. Don't get mad. You know we're just ready to brand. I need all the help I can get. You can't walk out on me now. I'll get you more money. Just keep it quiet, you understand? Don't let on to the rest of the crew. I'll go in right now. Just keep your shirt on."

Roscoe and Dink watched as Mosely hurried up the slope.

"He clean forgot to limp," Dink said and chuckled softly.

Two days later, with a promise from Mosely for a raise in wages, Roscoe and Dink got ready to start the long annual chore of branding the calf crop.

Chapter 9

THE WAGONS were loaded. The biggest one, the chuck
wagon, had the traditional canvas cover stretched over
hoops and a high cabinet which faced backward over
the tail gate. This cabinet held in its many drawers and
shelves all the kitchen condiments and essentials; when
the tail gate was up it covered the front of the cabinet,
when it was let down, and the folding legs drawn down,
the tail gate served as a table or counter in front of the
cabinet. Luke Stringer, the cook, rode the high seat at the
front of the chuck wagon, cursing his team.

"Hi! Come up! Lean into those collars! I'll be right
behind you."

With its high back and front and the canvas in between,
the chuck wagon resembled nothing so much as a minia-
ture of an old Spanish galleon.

The second wagon, called "the hoodlum," carried wood
and water and the bulky bedrolls belonging to the crew.
It was driven by Freddy, the kid, who helped the cook
hitch up, gathered wood, and helped the horse wrangler.

As the wagons rattled away from the corrals, the crew
were making their final preparations, tacking on horse-
shoes, checking their gear, and indulging in horseplay.

"I wonder," Dink said as he stretched a new stirrup
leather he had just put on his saddle, "I wonder if old
Luke's got any idea of where The Tubs camp is. He
ain't ever left the cook shack to go farther than the privy
to my knowledge."

"He'll find it," Roscoe said. "I told him how to go and
he can see those big black tanks ten miles off."

"I wouldn't count on it," Dink said. "That broken-down old bastard's got no sense of direction. You could lose him in a round corral with the gate shut."

"All you're worried about is your dinner," Roscoe said. "He'll have a meal waiting when we get there."

The saddle horses milled around in the big corral as the men finished their final preparations. A few hours after the wagons had pulled out the crew caught their horses and saddled up. The remuda was led out and the men surrounded them, shaping them into a herd. The horses ran, squealing and kicking for a ways, with the men in front holding them back by swinging the loopless ends of their ropes. After a bit the horses settled down and a herd was formed. They moved at a trot out across the flats, past the windmill in the horse pasture, past the last fence with its base of caught tumbleweeds woven into a thorny lace.

It was nearly sundown when they drove the horses into the water lot beside the big tarred tanks which gave the name to this camp and a whole section of range around it. "The Tubs." As Roscoe had predicted, dinner was ready.

After they had finished eating they helped the horse wrangler get the horses out on grass for the night. The first few nights they would be hard to hold, but after that they would settle down and never go far from the old bell mare. She was the only mare in the remuda, and the geldings were all devoted to her. As long as they could hear her bell they grazed quietly. At the wrangler's whistle she would start toward camp with the whole bunch at her heels.

"Well," Roscoe said as they climbed into their bedrolls that night, "vacation's over."

"Yeah," Dink said, "here goes the tallow I spent all winter storing up."

"Tallow?" Roscoe snorted. "If they rendered you for a month the only grease they'd get would be what's left of that junk you had the barber rub in your head last fall."

"O.K., O.K. Sign off. Mosely'll be getting us up in an hour or two," Dink said.

"Yeah," Roscoe said. "I never saw a man so proud of

the way he can get a crew out and have them standing around waiting for light enough to catch their horses."

"The sonofabitch must not be able to sleep any," Dink muttered from his bed. "He gets the rest of us up for company."

Roscoe cursed as he stumbled toward the fire. But, he told himself, you better get used to it. It'll be better than a month before we get that last one branded. Two men were already at the fire pouring coffee. Roscoe took a cup and was blowing into the black scalding brew when Dink joined him.

"What's the matter, Roscoe?" Dink said. "You're all humped up like a just bred cow. Not cold, are you?"

"No," Roscoe said, "I'm just getting ready to grab my ankles and make a hoop and roll away."

They stopped talking as the foreman came toward them silhouetted by the fire.

"Roscoe," Mosely said, "you know this country. How about running the gather?"

"Sure," Roscoe said.

"I'll stay in camp and get the gear organized and have the fires built when you come in with the cattle."

"No," Roscoe said, "I wouldn't build the fires till we get the herd set where we want to hold them."

"All right," Mosely said, "I'll just get things ready for you. This ankle is giving me hell."

Before they had finished eating and while it was still very dark, Roscoe heard the horses being brought in from the range. When they were ready the men went into the water lot and with several of them holding the ends of ropes they shaped a three-sided pen. The remuda were worked into this and the open side was closed on them.

Roscoe and Dink went in to catch the horses that would be wanted. As the cowboys called names to them they searched through the jumble of heads and backs for the mounts that were ordered. It was just light enough to silhouette heads against the graying sky. The horses were all well rope-broken and easy to hold up in a bunch. As the loops sailed over them they waited to see if they had been chosen, and if the rope did not settle on them they stood waiting or gently milling as the caught horse was led out.

Roscoe bent forward trying to skylight the herd. His rope was held with the big loop in his right hand and the slack spooled in his left. He spotted a familiar pair of ears and drew the loop over in front of himself and laid it on the ground on his left. When the ears appeared again he lifted the loop and stepped forward as he gave it one clockwise turn above his head. As he threw the loop he stepped toward the horses and paid out slack. When the loop dropped over the head of the horse he wanted, he jerked back on the rope with his right hand. Holding the rope high over his head so it would not be crossed by another horse, he tugged at it gently and the pony he had caught worked its way out of the bunch to him. Roscoe turned the horse over to the rider who had called for it, took his rope back, and turned to search the herd again.

Sometimes he threw a straight overhand loop, but most of the time he gave the rope one clockwise turn before letting it go. Occasionally his loop caught on a horse's ear or only fell across its neck, but by twitching the rope gently he could usually bring the horse out.

When all the men had their mounts, the "corral" was demolished and the wrangler took the remuda back to the grass, where he held them until a change of horses was wanted at noon.

The men began saddling and topping off their horses. Most of the range-bred ponies humped up and pitched in the cold morning air. Roscoe saddled and swung up easily onto the big savina horse Mosely had asked him to ride. He spun the horse quickly to the left and kept it spinning fast, chasing its tail, for several turns. Then he jerked the cow pony's head up and spurred him into a run out across the flat. Before the horse reached full stride and started to think about running away, Roscoe slid him to a stop and sent him running back the way he had come. By keeping him under constant watch and not giving him time to think or get his head, Roscoe had Figure Four warmed up before he had a chance to go to bucking.

Soon the others were mounted and ready. Roscoe headed out from camp at a long trot. He knew this range and knew where the cattle hung out. As they trotted along he was mapping the gather in his head.

When the sun came up, throwing a lot of light ahead of its promise of heat, Roscoe began scattering the riders. As the group passed a particular draw or trail, Roscoe would stand in his stirrups and wave his arm in the direction he wanted the man to take. One by one he sent the men off to both sides, and when only he and Dink were left he pulled his horse down for the first time since he had mounted. The roan savina settled gladly into a walk, blowing hard.

"Kee-rist!" Dink said, "that floating kidney of mine is up by my Adam's apple."

"What's the matter," Roscoe said with a grin, "don't you like a nice hard trot on a cold morning?"

"I wouldn't mind much if I was horseback," Dink said, "but this thing I've got my saddle on is a cross between one of those jackhammers they break up streets with and a riveting machine. How's Figure Four?"

"Smooth," Roscoe said. "Smooth as silk."

Roscoe reined in his horse and looked back the long canyon they had come up. They were at the head of the draw.

"Well," he said, "you want to take the south side?"

"Might just as well," Dink answered.

"See you in camp," Roscoe said and turned his pony up the hill.

When he got to the top of the ridge Roscoe surveyed the range below. In the light he could see all the way back to the tanks at camp. Below, the canyon they had come up widened out as it reached the plain and the brushy slopes flattened into one broad table. Roscoe started working his way over the rough ground back toward the camp. There was not a cow in sight.

Soon he kicked three cows and their calves out of a wash on the side of the ridge and sent them crashing through the brush and rocks down into the canyon. As the frantic cattle rushed down the slope they scared several more pairs of cows and calves out ahead of them. Roscoe studied the hillside and kept working his way along. Occasionally he made wide detours to shake out particular clumps of brush which he suspected might have cattle in them or to go up to the top and look around. On the other side of the canyon he saw the red cattle moving down and out of the gulches.

Once in a while he caught a glimpse of one of the other men working ahead of him. He noted when one of them was too low on the side of the hill, and when he reached that spot himself he would ride up and go through the area that man had missed. Ofter he surprised an old cow or two who had thought she was safely hidden and had been passed over.

The cattle spilled down the slope like an avalanche, and Roscoe reined up to watch them merge into a long column at the bottom of the draw.

Run, damn you, he was thinking, rattle your hocks.

He turned toward the end of the ridge and kicked his horse into a lope. Now he had to get down to the flat and make a herd out of them before they could separate and scatter or turn in the wrong direction. His pony slowed to flounder through some loose rocks, and Roscoe cursed at the delay. The ground dropped away, and Roscoe sent the big savina sliding stiff-legged down through the shale. The cattle were pouring out onto the plain below, and two riders were swinging around them turning the leaders.

"Head them!" Roscoe shouted, knowing that he could not be heard. "Head them and hold them!"

He leaned back with his rein hand held high and the other hand braced against the saddle swells as his horse slid, stumbled, and jumped down the steep grade. When he got the chance to look toward the cattle again Roscoe saw a rider dive into a wash going too fast. The pony tumbled and the rider was thrown free. The man held fast to his reins, and Roscoe saw him jump back onto the horse as soon as it was on its feet.

Other riders emerged from adjacent draws pushing

smaller groups of cattle in front of them, and soon the flat was covered with hundreds of bawling, milling cows and calves. Dink galloped over to Roscoe and shouted above the din.

"Where you been? I had my side clean a hour ago."

Roscoe grinned at him and sat his horse, studying the animals.

"Tell the boys," he shouted, "to hold them here and let them mother up."

Dink nodded and wheeled his horse to go tell the rest of the crew. Roscoe watched as the men moved away from the herd, allowing the cattle to spread out. The cows moved busily from calf to calf, sniffing each one and bellowing toward the hills. The calves stood spraddle-legged, bawling steadily.

As the herd spread out, there was more room for the cows to work among the calves and gradually they paired up again. The calves ducked under their mothers and, with their white-tipped tails flicking from side to side, nursed eagerly. The uproar diminished and then ceased except for an occasional restless bugle from one of the cows.

Roscoe sat his horse patiently, and when a few of the calves lay down in the shade beneath their mothers Roscoe stood in his stirrups and waved his hand in a circle over his head. The riders moved slowly in on the cattle and Roscoe swung around the herd to point them up toward camp.

When they reached the flat near their camp, they turned the herd back upon itself and milled them into a bunch. Roscoe waved the men back and once again the pairs mothered up. While half the crew held the herd, the other half loped toward the wagons to change horses and eat. It was after twelve.

"It looks like a good gather, Roscoe," Mosely said as Roscoe brought his loaded plate away from the collection of Dutch ovens and squatted on his heels in the shade of the wagon.

Roscoe nodded, his mouth full of biscuit.

"Better than three hundred cows," he mumbled.

"I have three sets of irons laid out," Mosely said, "I'll get those fires going. How many ropers do you think it will take to feed calves to three fires?"

"Let me and Dink rope. That'll be enough."

"Fine," the foreman said. "If you get behind I'll come help you."

Dink, who had come up with his plate full of food just in time to catch this last remark, choked on his coffee, cursed, and hurried away. When he returned Mosely had gone to see to the starting of the fires.

" 'I'll come out and help you,' " Dink mimicked. "Deliver me from that."

"Maybe you and me ought to stay at a fire," Roscoe said, "flanking or something. Let him rope. Watch the fun."

They ate hurriedly, caught up fresh horses, and loped out to the herd and relieved the other riders, who went in to change horses and eat. When the whole crew was assembled at the herd once more, Roscoe rode away from the group gathered around Mosley. He's the boss now he was thinking. He'll take over and give lots of orders. Mosely, walking with an exaggerated limp, distributed the men at the three fires and sent the rest of the riders out to help hold the herd. Roscoe shook out a small loop in his rope and watched the crews at the fires.

"Ready?" he asked Dink.

Dink shoved a fresh wad of snuff behind his lower lip.

"Ready as I'll ever get," Dink said and spat copiously.

"I kind of hate to start," Dink said when he had gotten the snoose settled where it belonged. "Once we commence it's going to be a long time afore we can quit."

"Why don't we just forget about branding this year?" Roscoe said. "Let's let them go and sit back and watch the neighbors fight over them."

"Good idea," Dink said.

They reined their horses toward the herd and, holding the loops in their ropes up shoulder high, they rode slowly into the bunch of cattle who parted in front of them. Roscoe raised his hand and flipped his loop down and caught a calf. He turned his horse and, moving slowly but steadily, made his way out of the herd toward the first fire.

As he brought the calf, bucking and bawling to the fire, the two flankers stepped out to meet him. One of the men caught the calf by the tail while the other reached across its back and grabbed it by the neck with one hand and the loose hide of its flank with the other. The flanker rolled the calf against his legs, lifting all four of the little animal's feet off the ground, and then dropped him on his side. Roscoe stopped his horse.

The man who had been holding the calf's tail let it go and grabbed the calf's hind foot. He pulled back on the uppermost hind foot with both hands and stretched it toward himself as he put his foot on the hock of the other hind leg and sat down pushing the lower leg forward, away from himself. Holding the hind legs this way secured the calf and at the same time exposed the testicles of the bulls, which had to be cut off.

The flanker, in the meantime, had knelt on the calf's neck and bent the top foreleg back. When he had the calf firmly held he slipped Roscoe's rope off and Roscoe headed for the herd, building a new loop. Dink was coming toward him with a big heifer calf which he had caught by the hind legs. The calf was sliding along, bawling back toward the herd.

"Getting kind of fancy, huh?" Roscoe said as they passed.

"Naw," Dink said, "but those jokers can't flank them this big without straining a gut so I thought I'd make it easy for them."

Roscoe looked back and saw the third crew waiting around the fire. All right, he said to himself, if it's cattle you want I'm the boy that can give them to you.

He and Dink dragged the calves out of the seething herd one by one. One by one the men at the fires flanked them, castrated the bulls, notched ears, vaccinated, gouged out the little horn buttons, and laid on the hot irons. A cloud of bitter smoke rose from each calf as it was branded, and the calf always bawled and tried to kick free.

Often when one of the little calves was finished and turned loose, instead of going back to the herd it would dash away toward the hills, thinking to find its mother there. Every time one of these calves struck out, the cows on the fringe of the herd, who had all lost their calves by now, would bellow toward the escaping calf and press out to follow. The men holding the herd rode back and forth against them, turning them in.

The dust grew thicker and rose lazily and hung in the air. The din was constant. Coming back from the fire now, Roscoe could not see the herd for the dust. He breathed through his nose until it plugged solid and then he had to breathe through his mouth. The dirt collected on his teeth and lips and the taste of it filled his mouth. His lips cracked and bled, and the blood coagulated with the dust and the cracks lengthened. The dust collected in the corners of his squinting eyes and formed hard little balls. The heat grew more intense. Louder and louder the cattle bawled.

"I think," Roscoe said as he rode up to Mosely who was keeping the tally, "I think you better shut down that third fire and put the crew to holding herd. Slick-eared calves are getting scarce and the cows are getting pretty ringy."

"All right," the foreman said. "You don't think there's any danger of losing the bunch of them, do you?"

"It's happened before," Roscoe said and drew his bandanna up over his nose and mouth again as he turned back to the dust cloud the cattle were stirring up.

He met Dink, who was sitting on his horse outside of the herd.

"I told them to back off a minute," Dink said. "They're really going on the prod."

Roscoe nodded and relaxed beside his partner.

"I told Mosely the Miser we could lose them," Roscoe said, pulling down his bandanna. "Told him to put the third fire out."

"Yeah," Dink said, "It's taking longer to find the calves now. We must be pretty near done. Say, if we lost the bunch now, wouldn't that be hell? We'd have to make the whole gather again."

"Uh huh," Roscoe answered, "and you just try to find some of those old smart cows tomorrow if they do get away from us. They'll take their calves so far back in the brush that they'll be yearlings before they find their way out."

"You bet," Dink said.

Roscoe pulled up his bandanna again and rode into the dust. He raised his hand, holding the loop high, and worked easily into the milling cattle. Finally he found an unbranded calf, and as it crossed in front of his horse he flipped his loop and rolled it over the calf's back so that the loop swung back toward him under the calf. At the touch of the rope the calf leaped forward and its hind feet stepped neatly into the open noose. Roscoe jerked his slack and turned to work his way out of the herd. As he came into the open, dragging the calf behind, several of the distraught cows tried to follow the calf out, their heads down, sniffing at the captive. The herd guards closed in from either side and turned them back.

An hour later, just as the sun was settling on the rimrock to the west and sending out the blue and orange and yellow light which spread all across the sky, Dink and Roscoe decided that all the calves were marked. The crew from one of the fires was sent in to look, and when they reported they could not find any calves with their ears intact, the word was given and the riders backed away from the cattle, who dispersed quickly with a great deal of bawling and bellowing.

Gradually they found each other, and the cows made a great to-do of licking and nuzzling their mutilated calves. The calves themselves showed much more concern over getting their supper than they did for their wounds. Gradually the flat cleared as the pairs trotted off toward the breaks. The men rode slowly to camp and unsaddled. It was nearly eight o'clock. They had been up since three.

"Oh for the life of a cowboy!" Dink said as he washed in the trough beside one of the big tanks.

"You bet," Roscoe said as he gently sloshed water against his cracked lips. "*You* bet."

Luke, the cook, rattled the coal-covered lids off the black Dutch ovens and the men began straggling toward the fire. Dink came back from the trough, singing:

> *I've traveled up and I've traveled down,*
> *I've traveled this country round and round,*
> *I've lived in cities, I've lived in towns,*
> *But I've got this much to say:*
> *Before you try cow punching kiss your wife,*
> *Take a heavy insurance on your life,*
> *Then cut your throat with a Bowie knife,*
> *For it's easier done that way.*

The familiar old song drew a few smiles from the tired men who were busily helping themselves to supper of thin steaks and thick biscuits.

"Huh," snorted Luke. "I know a better one than that."

Going into a shuffling little dance that lifted the skirt of his flour-sack apron, Luke croaked:

> *The cook's an unfortunate son of a gun,*
> *He has to be up 'fore the rise of the sun,*
> *His language is awful, his curses are deep,*
> *He's just like cascara, he works while you sleep.*

And so it went for six weeks as they moved from one part of the range to another, until the wagons returned to headquarters and a number of the men were let go. Roscoe and Dink were among the hands who drew their last pay.

"Should've quit two months ago," Dink said.

"Yeah," Roscoe said, "but that would put us in the same class with that Mosely. He'd swear we walked out on him when he needed us. He'd say we were undependable and so on. I don't want to give the likes of him a chance to bitch about me."

"Well," Dink said, "it's been one helluva long time

between drinks and I'm looking for a real lubrication. Do you suppose they've got any whiskey left in town?"

"Wouldn't surprise me."

"A good soak in a tub is going to feel good, too," Dink said. "And tomorrow I aim to sleep till noon. I'm purely wore out. My old piles are dragging so every time I wipe myself it feels like I'm shaking hands with somebody."

"Hell, Dink," Roscoe said. "You're a young man yet. What are you going to do when you're as old and broke down as me?"

"I'll never make it," Dink said, shaking his head. "The good die young, you know."

They spent four rowdy days in town and then split up. Dink went to work with a movie crew shooting on location in the badlands east of town and Roscoe headed for California.

"Why California?" Dink asked.

"Want to see what it's like," Roscoe said.

Chapter 10

ROSCOE SPENT two years in California working on ranches in the central part of the state. At one point he found himself working for the first time under the direction of a young man who had no experience beyond what a four-year course in animal husbandry at a state college had provided him.

The owner of the ranch, a wealthy oil man who used the cattle to better his tax position, seldom visited the place. He came down in the spring to watch the calves branded and on the afternoon of the last day of branding invited the men over to his ornate Spanish-style house for a drink.

"That's over for another year," Earl said as they rode into the corral.

"Yeah," the other member of the crew said, "and I'm not sorry."

Hell, Roscoe thought, you two don't know what hard work is. He jerked his saddle off the deep-chested quarter horse he had been riding and made for the tack room. Professional gripers, he thought, that's what those two are. They've been moaning all winter and spring about everything they've had to do. Not that some of the ideas that Forrest comes up with aren't enough to turn a man's milk, but what can you expect from a kid who learned everything he knows out of a book?

"Come on," Earl called. "The boss wants us at the big house."

They walked across the graveled road toward the low stucco house. The boss was standing on the veranda with his manager in the purple shade. They had glasses in their hands. Roscoe ran his tongue over his cracked lips.

"Hi, boys," the boss called heartily. "Come wet your whistles."

The afternoon sun slanted under the eaves onto the porch and they took their chairs around the wheeled table which was laden with glasses, bottles, and a pail of ice.

"What's yours, Roscoe?" the big, genial ranch owner asked.

Ice rattled in the glasses and the whiskey cut the dusty taste in his throat as Roscoe sipped.

"Well," the boss was saying, "how do you think it went? I mean, Forrest here and I were just talking it over, wondering if there was any way we could have improved on the branding operation this year. I say it went off very well. Of course, I didn't see much of it, but what I saw impressed me."

They were all nodding, so Roscoe told himself to let it ride. Johnny and Earl had plenty of complaints out there but now they were agreeing with everything. Sure, they like their jobs and want to keep them, but why don't they sound off with some of the stuff they've been crying to me about?

"How about last winter?" the boss asked. "I wasn't here a great deal of the time. Forrest tells me that you boys did splendidly keeping the cows bunched for the bulls. We should have a fine, even calf crop next year. How could we improve on that system?"

Now, Roscoe was thinking, now they'll sing.

He remembered how the young manager had made them ride the slick, wet hills of the ranch all winter, driving the cows into groups on the range so that the bulls would be sure to get them all. They had driven the little newborn calves up and down the steep hills with the cows. The calves had lost their mothers, and Roscoe wondered how many of them had failed to mother up again. The two regular hands had complained bitterly about the system. As a newcomer Roscoe had kept his opinions to himself and gone on doing what he was told. The boss signed the checks, and if this was the way he wanted it done he would do it that way.

But he felt that the policy was foolish. He knew that the bulls and cows would find each other. He knew that the older bulls would hang out around the watering places and wait for the cows to come in to drink. And just as surely, the young bulls would rush around the hills seeking cows in heat. He thought about the old wheeze in which an old bull and a young one look down into a valley and see a herd of heifers. "Gee," said the young bull, "let's run down there and breed a couple of them." "Better still," answered the old bull, "let's *walk* down and breed them *all*."

The owner waited for comment from the men, and when none was forthcoming he went on.

"I admit that we had some trouble rotating the bulls, but I think it paid off."

Hell, Roscoe was thinking, how could it pay? It had been a joke. The bulls, all purebred, had little numbers branded on their horns. On the first day of the year those bulls with even numbers on their horns had been turned out with the cows, and the plan was to bring them in after a week to be fed up while the other half was turned out. After a month of this Forrest had ordered all the bulls turned out. The young bulls began to lose flesh, but instead of letting the men pick out those they thought needed feeding the manager called for all the even-numbered bulls to be brought in. It was impossible. The bulls had been rubbing their horns in the muddy earth and the numbers were beyond reading even when you could get close to them, which was not often.

"Help yourselves, boys," the boss was saying. "I want you to feel free to tell me everything you can think of that might improve our system."

Why don't they talk? Roscoe asked himself. They've been riding around all winter beefing about the way this spread is run.

"How about all the trouble we had," the boss went on, "when we were trying to mother up after separating the heifers from the bull calves? That seemed awkward to me. Forrest and I were just talking it over. Can you think of any way to make it easier?"

Hell yes, Roscoe thought, but you're not asking me. I'm just temporary here and you wouldn't listen if I told you. But great cow-sucking jackrabbits, I've never seen such a mess as trying to mother those calves. Everybody working against everybody else and the damn fool of a Forrest charging around in the middle.

Earl and Johnny were shaking their heads solemnly.

"No way around it, I reckon," Johnny said.

Why, for chrissake, Roscoe wanted to say, you jokers are supposed to be cowhands. If you never worked on any outfits that were run smarter than this one I guess you just never had a chance to learn. Me and any three one-legged Mexicans could make you guys look like so many girl scouts.

"Well," the owner was saying, "it still seems to me that we could avoid some of the confusion."

"I think, A.J.," Forrest said, "that I have a plan which will prove more efficient. We'll have a try next year."

The boss smiled and nodded and Roscoe thought: Yes, you've got a whole year to come up with something, Junior. Maybe you can get a book from some college that has a chapter in it about how to handle cattle. You've got books on about everything else in that office of yours.

"Drink up, boys," the owner said. "Drink up. The big job is over. Time to relax now."

They refilled their glasses. Good bourbon, anyway, Roscoe thought, can't complain about that. But this is no place for a hillbilly like me. Best I get back where they got ranches that would use this whole place for a calf pasture. Those drinks taste like more. Maybe I can talk Forrest into paying me off tonight.

One of the California ranches he worked on raised Thoroughbred horses as a sideline. When Roscoe left there he took with him a shiny bay colt as part of his wages. Soldier, he named him, and for many years Roscoe and the big bay horse were almost inseparable. It was on this ranch that he went through a particularly unpleasant ordeal.

The owners, two brothers who had taken over after their father's death, had bought six hundred yearling heifers with a view toward pasturing them until fall and then fattening them in a feedlot. One day as Roscoe rode through the gently rolling hills where these heifers were pastured he found a stillborn calf on the grass under an oak tree. This meant only one thing: one of the heifers had been bred and since they all came from the same ranch any number of the rest of them could be carrying calves. The next day the men rode through the herd looking for signs of pregnancy in the yearlings.

<We came up with a whole slug of them, and we found more later. The next couple of months were gen-u-wine hell. Those little heifers couldn't get themselves from around their calves. We worked day and night pulling calves. Sometimes we'd get a calf out of one of them alive, but not often, and most of the time when we did the heifer would jump up and run off and have nothing to do with the calf we took out of her. Sometimes we just couldn't pull the calf out of them any way at all

and we'd have to go in and cut it up and bring it out in pieces. Not much fun.>

The rodeo game now played a large part in Roscoe's life. As a young man, before rodeos had become the organized exhibitions of highly specialized skills that they are today, Roscoe and men like him played at them for fun and later worked at them for money. The early-day rodeos were often slapdash affairs without firm sets of rules and were sometimes blatantly dishonest. A contest would be advertised and prizes announced, but the results were subject to manipulation and the prize money reduced by "unforeseen expenses."

<There was this one little show about halfways between the two big ones. I had to make enough of a stake to raise my entry fees for the next big one so I drifted on over and signed up in damn near every event they offered. You could tell they were kind of hostile to strangers, but they were real white about the whole thing to let me in.>

The day of the show Roscoe stood behind the chutes and watched the bucking horses run in. The familiar smells of horses, cattle, and dust pervaded the sunny afternoon. Colorfully shirted cowboys stood in small groups nodding to one another as they inspected the chute full of bucking horses. Roscoe stood apart, a stranger in their midst. The partitions were slid in, shutting the broncs in their individual chutes, and Roscoe climbed up to inspect the horse he had drawn. It was a big pinto with feet the size of stove lids. Roscoe eased his saddle down onto the broad back and climbed back down the chute.

One of the youngsters helping at the chutes loped past.

"You got a hook?" Roscoe asked, and the boy looked up and down the row of chutes.

"There was three or four of them here a minute ago," the boy said nervously.

Hell, Roscoe thought, he acts like he was going to ride this nag instead of me.

"I'll wait till somebody's through with one," he said, and the boy hurried on his way.

That's the trouble with these little shows, he thought, but what the hell. He looked across the arena at the warped grandstand of rough green-painted boards. Not much of a crowd and all locals from the way they've been yelling at the ropers. A calf leaped out of the roping chute and a rider on a buckskin horse charged out of the barrier.

"Get him, Jimmy," someone shouted from the stands.

Jimmy missed, and since he did not have a second loop made up he reined in his horse hard and rode back to the gate, spooling his rope and shaking his head. When he got to the gate he jerked at the buckskin's mouth with three savage tugs.

"That's right," Roscoe muttered, "punish your horse because you can't rope."

Roscoe took time out from watching the ropers to find a straightened coat hanger with a hook bent in one end. He reached through the slats of the chute and hooked the cinch ring hanging on the far side of the big pinto and drew it under the horse's belly. When he had finished tightening the cinch he turned again to watch the ropers. Roscoe had roped in the first section and was interested to see if his time would be worth any money. A roper sailed out and caught his calf only a few feet from the barrier. The little brown horse squatted and slid perfectly as the boy bailed off into the dust.

"Go, Dave!" came from the stands.

The boy ran to the calf but Roscoe did not watch him; he was studying the little brown horse as it backed against the rope. He's taking too long to tie him, but that pony is sure working, Roscoe was thinking when he heard a groan go up from the crowd. He looked and saw the calf kick loose and jump to its feet and the flagman wave "no time."

Well, he thought, I still stand second in the calf roping. The crowd is sure rooting for the home guards. I wonder if the judges will let an outsider like me win the bronc riding?

The first two horses out unloaded their riders without

much difficulty, and then it was Roscoe's turn. He eased himself down onto the pinto until his feet found the stirrups; then he measured the single bucking rein and choked up on it. Everything felt right as he scrunched his hips forward and back, getting his seat. The horse was trembling but it stood quietly with its head lowered.

This old pony has been around, Roscoe was thinking. He'll likely come out good, clear the chutes, and go to bucking. He swung his feet up forward so that he was beyond the points of the horse's shoulders with his spurs. It's all how you start them, he thought; you've got to bring them out strong. Well, I'm the boy that can do it. The judges were standing on either side of the chute now with their big scorecards. They were on his left since the gate opened in that direction.

"Unchain him," Roscoe said, nodding to one of the local men who was working the chutes.

Now, Roscoe said to himself, now, you hillbillies, this is how it should be done.

At the first movement of the chute gate he lifted his right foot and drove his spur into the pinto's shoulder with all his strength. The gate swung away to the left and the horse surged away from the biting spur. Roscoe sunk in both spurs and leaned back for the lunge he knew was coming, but at that instant the gate stopped swinging although it was only a third open. The horse crashed into the heavy gate, mashing Roscoe's left leg against the rough lumber. Then the gate swung wide and the horse regained his balance and lunged again out into the arena.

Roscoe's left leg was numb and he had no idea whether or not that foot was still in the stirrup, but since there seemed to be nothing else to do he began spurring and balancing, leaning and raking ahead of the strides of the big bronc. The dirty no-good sonofabitch, he said to himself, as he took each pile-driving jolt and spurred harder. The horse bucked well, and when the whistle blew the pickup men were quick to come in. Roscoe grabbed for the rider on his left when he felt the rein being taken away from him. He swung over the back of the pickup pony and slid to the ground, being careful to take his weight on his right foot. He limped back to the judges, testing his leg. It was not broken, but the knee felt mushy and weak. The judges were huddled together nodding at one another.

"How about a reride?" Roscoe said.

"What for?" the taller of the two asked.

"For getting that gate checked on me," Roscoe said.

"I didn't see any gate get checked," the tall one said.

"We goose-egged you because you were coasting with your left foot when you brought him out," the shorter judge said.

"You didn't see him block that gate?" Roscoe asked, scowling and jerking his thumb toward the man at the chutes.

"No," said the tall judge, looking him in the eye.

Roscoe stared at him for a moment and then shrugged. "Well," he said, "you're going to have to pay off on the calf roping, or are you going to claim the clocks were wrong?"

"Just a minute, you," the short judge began, but Roscoe turned away and limped out of the arena. He collected what he could that night, loaded Soldier in the trailer behind the cut-down Model A, and drove north without even stopping to buy supper.

"To hell with them," he muttered. "Here I'll be crippling around for a week and those lousy farmers will be telling each other how good their local boys are. To hell with them." Anger prodding him, he drove on through the night and did not stop until he had put many miles behind. When he did stop it was at a little mining town built on the side of a steep mountain. The lower section of the single serpentine street glowed with neon signs, and Roscoe made short work of finding a place to stable his horse.

His temper had subsided a little by the time he swung a leg over an imitation leather stool in one of the dim little bars. The place was not crowded and the patrons seemed as bored as the fat glass-polishing bartender. Roscoe downed two shots before he began to relax. I wish, he was thinking, that I was the kind that could buy a ten-cent magazine and just go to bed. I come into a town and I got to look around a little like I was scared I might miss something. When you get to looking you generally find something and then things get expensive.

He sipped at his whiskey until it was gone, and then he put the glass down and brushed his fingers on the bar toward himself, palm down the way he called for another card when he was playing blackjack and said, "Hit me again," to the bloated bartender. There was a brunette at the back end of the bar perched on a stool playing with some sort of a pink drink. The bartender poured and Roscoe tossed off the shot in one gulp. "Once again," he said, shoving the glass and some money across the bar. and slid onto the stool next to the brunette.

"Hi," Roscoe said.

"Hi, yourself, cowboy," she said, smiling.

Roscoe opened his eyes and without knowing how he had gotten there realized that he was in jail. He closed his eyes quickly and tried to go back to sleep but it was no use. He rolled over and sat up as gently as he could. God, what a hangover. I think I could patent this one; nobody ever had a head like this. He sat on the edge of the bunk with his head in his hands trying to recall the night before, trying to remember the name of the town. His mind kept running back to the rodeo of the day before.

"Hey," he called and heard the legs of a chair hit the cement floor at the end of the corridor. A tall, lean man with a long horsey face appeared at the cell door, unlocking it.

"Well, cowboy," he said, smiling, "you had yourself quite a time."

"If you say so," Roscoe groaned. "Give me the details."

"I wasn't on when they brought you in," he said, "but they tell me you were determined to sleep on the county."

"Am I booked?"

"No, they just wanted to get you out of circulation. Said

they took you across the tracks twice but you kept coming back."

"I'm one smart sonofabitch," Roscoe said.

"Took you down to the barn where your horse and outfit was, but you damn near beat them back up to Main Street."

"Good for me."

"You can leave when you want. If I was you I'd slope on out of town, though," the tall jailer said.

"Thanks. Can I stop long enough for a shave?"

"You bet. Nobody's mad."

"Good," Roscoe said and stood up very carefully.

Chapter 11

JIM DUNCAN found Roscoe eating dinner in the Black Cat Café:

"How've you been, Roscoe?" Jim asked as he slid his bulky frame into the booth across from Roscoe.

"Just right."

"Cris at the saddle shop told me you were in town. How about judging the bronc riding for us this year?"

"I sort of figured on entering myself," Roscoe said, lying but not even admitting to himself that it was a lie.

"Like to have you judge for us," Big Jim said, helping himself to a roll. "Perry Adams will work with you."

"How does it pay?"

"A hundred and a quarter," Jim said. "That's the best we can do."

"That's better than paying a entry fee to ride and then bucking off," Roscoe said with a grin.

"Yeah," Jim said. "You can still rope if you want to. You got that Soldier horse?"

"Couldn't do without him," Roscoe said.

"He's a lot of horse," Jim said and paused. "How about it?"

"I guess I might as well," Roscoe said. "I hate to do it though. Never made any friends judging yet."

"I know," Jim said.

"Who are you getting the stock from this year?"

"Hank Bartlett is furnishing the horses, and we're getting the rope stock from around locally," Jim said. "Hank wanted the whole show but he was asking too much money."

"What kind of a string has old Hank got now?"

"Well," Jim said, "I saw his horses work down south. They were kind of tired. He claims he'll have some fresh ones for us, but that's not saying he will."

"Yeah," Roscoe said. "Well, if I can get a partner I'll come over tomorrow and sign up for the team roping."

"Swell," Jim said. "I'll see you around."

Jim left and Roscoe finished his meal. I guess it's for the best, he told himself. Maybe I can get Clancy to heel for me in the team roping.

Roscoe held the big piece of cardboard which had the names of the riders and the broncs they had drawn on it and chewed on the stub of a pencil the rodeo announcer had loaned him. The calf roping was almost over and the saddle bronc riding was next up. Roscoe watched the roper who was in the arena.

I don't like this, he was thinking, I don't like any part of it, but I'm stuck so there's nothing to do now. I should have turned them down when they first asked me to judge this show. I know too many of the boys who are riding and I'm sure not going to be able to make them all happy. Oh well, I need the dough and if I wasn't down here judging I'd be riding myself, and I'm better off down here.

He looked over the list of riders and broncs. He knew all but two of the boys entered and he had seen or ridden all of the horses. As he studied the list he heard the announcer tell the crowd that the next event was going to be the saddle bronc riding. Roscoe went over to the chutes and smiled at Perry Adams, the other judge.

"We aren't going to make any friends today, Perry," he said.

"Hell, Roscoe," tough old Perry grumbled. "I been judging so long I ain't got a friend left."

Roscoe nodded and they separated so that one would be on either side of the first horse as he came out. The boy, Bill Woolworth, was set and Roscoe saw him nod his head at the man on the chute gate. The gate opened and Bill spurred his mount, a big blue roan named Blucher, out into the arena. Roscoe watched Bill's feet. He crouched and backed away as the horse exploded into action.

Pretty good, Roscoe was thinking as he watched, pretty good. He started him right, brought old Blucher out clean with his spurs way up in the shoulders and from what I saw he kept his spurs working right along. Old Blucher isn't such a tough horse to sit, though. He bucks pretty straight away. I'll score the horse forty out of a hundred and I'll give Bill seventy. That's a hundred and ten. A man can't win much on an easy horse like Blucher, but he can make a pretty ride. I'll bet Perry scores it higher because he never rode Blucher. He had quit riding before that horse was even foaled.

The next horse out bucked off his rider, and Roscoe drew a big zero next to the boy's name. The rider came limping back and shook his head at Roscoe.

"Goose-egged again, Roscoe," he said. "I ought to quit."

"You can't expect to ride 'em all," Roscoe said.

He turned back to the chutes in time to see a black horse pawing up over one of the closed gates. The rider, one of the boys Roscoe did not know, was trying vainly to get the horse back down in the chute. Two of the hands who were working for the show were attempting to help.

"Are you ready, Larry?" Roscoe called to a red-headed boy at the end of the chutes. The boy nodded.

"All right," Roscoe turned to the announcer's stand, "take Larry Holmes out of four, Bob."

"Larry Holmes," the loudspeaker blared, "out of chute number four on Who Cares."

Who Cares stalled in the chute when the gate was opened, and Roscoe could see Larry spurring him, but the horse just hung his head and sulled. Someone behind the chutes poked a stick through and jabbed Who Cares and he jumped stiff-legged out into the arena and began to spin around in tight circles. Larry had to keep his inside spur buried behind the horse's front leg to keep from being spun off. The whistle blew and the pickup men went in to take him off.

No score, Roscoe said to himself, tough luck. We ought to give him a reride, but we won't because if he had used both feet he would have gotten points. They ought to chicken that horse.

The next rider put on quite a show. His horse bucked straight away but it had a vicious way of twisting its back which made him hard to sit. The rider was raking his feet back and forth very fast like a bicycle rider. It was pretty.

Roscoe found Perry standing beside him as they watched the horse and rider going down the arena away from them.

"Nice ride," Perry was saying.

"Yeah," Roscoe said, "but he's just polishing his boots on that horse. Look how his spurs are turned straight back. He ain't scratching, he's just rubbing."

"You're right," Perry said. "I guess old Murphy has been in this game long enough to learn all the tricks."

"Yeah," Roscoe said, "he's taking no chances and from the stands it looks like he's a world beater."

When the pickup men swung in and took Murphy off his horse the crowd cheered enthusiastically.

"Go ahead and yell," Roscoe said as he wrote down his score, "but it won't help his total."

He gave the horse eighty points and the rider forty. A hundred twenty, he was thinking; not much. If he had taken a chance and really spurred he could have scored a hundred sixty easy. Yeah, and he could have bucked off.

A pinto horse came next with Jerry Hunt on it. The pinto squealed as Jerry spurred, and the crowd laughed. Roscoe could hear Jerry's spur rowels whirring as he raked the pitching horse.

"That's the way to do it," Roscoe said aloud to no one. "You don't need to look see if Jerry's using his gut hooks, you can hear him. Too bad he didn't draw a better bronc."

The pinto was tapering off and then he stopped bucking and went into a spin. The pickup men anticipated the whistle and closed in on him. The pinto stopped and threw up its head an instant before the whistle blew. Too bad, Roscoe thought. He scored the horse forty points and Jerry ninety.

"He overrode him, eh, Roscoe?" Perry said.

Roscoe nodded.

"The pickups went in too soon, too," Roscoe said. "If he asks for a reride do we give him one?"

Perry shrugged and said, "I don't think they hurt him. That horse just figured he'd had enough."

O.K., Roscoe was thinking, but I'd say Jerry had a legitimate beef.

Jerry gimped up to Roscoe.

"How about it?" the bronc rider said.

"Can't help you, Jerry," Roscoe said. "They ought to get rid of that gutless wonder, though."

Jerry looked at Roscoe for a long minute and then turned away. Roscoe watched him go back to the chutes shaking his head. I don't blame you, Roscoe said to himself, but that's the way the world turns.

They gave only one reride that day, and that was when a bronc fell with his rider.

"Pretty sorry, huh, Roscoe?" Clancy growled in his gravelly baritone.

"Worse than that," Roscoe said as he tightened the cinches on his big bay rope horse.

Roscoe sat on Soldier and watched the first teams come out and rope. The horse flicked his ears back and forth and shifted his weight nervously. Roscoe dropped a hand to the big horse's neck, steadying him.

When it was their turn he and Clancy rode to the

barrier together and parted at the chute. Roscoe went into the slot on one side of the chute and Clancy swung in on the other side. Soldier fidgeted for a moment and then stood poised. Roscoe nodded and saw their steer leap out toward the handicap line. Soldier charged after it, and Roscoe rose in his stirrups. As he let go of the loop he knew it was wrong.

The steer swept under it, and Roscoe reined Soldier to one side. They were allowed three loops in total to catch the steer by both ends, so Clancy overrode Roscoe and neatly caught the steer around the neck. By the time that Clancy had spun the steer around, Roscoe had built a new loop and was in position to catch the hind legs. He rolled his loop out so that it slapped the steer across the legs. The steer stepped into the noose, and Roscoe rode away.

Roscoe was so disgusted and angry that he left the arena as quickly as he could. He did not want to see or talk to anyone. Once Soldier was in his stall and fed, Roscoe drove away and did not appear in town that night.

The next day he showed up just in time to take his place with Perry in front of the chutes. The horses were the same ones used the day before, with only a few exceptions, and the results were much the same. When he was through he went to where he had tied Soldier to the fence. Clancy rode over to him.

"Do you think we ought to swap ends, Roscoe?" Clancy asked.

Roscoe was spooling up his ropes and putting them into the round galvanized can he kept them in.

"You mean you head and me heel?" he asked, straightening up.

"Yeah," Clancy said. "Maybe we'd do better."

"I don't know," Roscoe said. "I missed yesterday, but I feel lucky today."

Clancy shrugged and walked away. Roscoe finished putting away his extra ropes and shook out a loop in the one he intended to use in the team roping which was the next event. I guess, he was thinking, it's time for me and Clancy to part company. He's a good heeler when he wants to be, but as long as he's thinking he's going to have to take the head when I miss he isn't worth anything.

Roscoe went to where he had Soldier tied to the arena fence and put the rope on his saddle.

When the starter told him that he and Clancy were next up but one, he rode down to the barrier and looked in to see what kind of a steer they had drawn. It was a lean-flanked roan with good horns. Just the right kind, Roscoe was thinking, just right for a flat fast loop.

When his turn came, Roscoe backed Soldier into the barrier and watched the starter fasten the elastic across in front, closing him in. The steer was shoved and hot-shotted up into the chute. Roscoe saw that Clancy had placed himself in the barrier on the other side of the chute. He was hoping that he would come out strong. If, Roscoe was thinking, he's playing me to catch the head he will come out hard so he'll be in a good position when I jerk that steer for him. If he's figuring that I'll likely miss, he will come out behind me so when I miss he can go for the head. Coming out late that way, if I do catch he'll be a day late and a dollar short getting up to where he can catch the hind legs and we never will win any money.

"Ready, Roscoe?" the boy on the chute called.

"Turn him go," Roscoe said.

The double gate on the front of the chute snapped open and the boy jammed his hot shot into the steer's rump. The big roan leaped out of the cage and stretched out into stride. When the steer's front feet touched the white line out in front of the chute, Roscoe saw the starter's flag begin to move down and he let Soldier go. The big horse jumped forward and the barrier sprang away from in front of his chest just before he reached it.

The steer was lined out just right, and Roscoe flipped his loop twice before he shot it out toward the bobbing horns. The loop settled flat onto the horns, and before it had a chance to drop over the steer's nose Roscoe jerked it back, tightening the loop right around the base of the curved horns.

When the steer reached the end of the rope, he was jerked around and in so doing his hind feet were thrown into the air. There, Roscoe thought, that's when you should have had your loop out, Clancy. We'd have first money sure, but where are you, you're loping along behind waiting to see if I'll catch him or not so you're going to make me turn and drag him for you and we will be slow time for sure.

Soldier leaned against the drag of the rope, and as Roscoe took the steer away Clancy rolled his loop in under the animal. The loop stood upright for a moment and then slapped across the steer's hind legs, and as the loop was settling the steer stepped into it and Clancy jerked the rope tight. As the steer hit the ground, the flagman signaled time. They took Roscoe's rope off and he rode out of the arena.

"Good catch, Roscoe," one of the contestants said.

"What was our time?" Roscoe asked.

"Fifteen two."

"Where does that make us stand?"

"You're second so far."

"Good," Roscoe said and rode to the fence where his rope can lay.

"If that old maid of a Clancy had of been there, we'd be standing first safe," he told Soldier as he loosened the cinches. "Yes," he went on, "and if I had caught that steer yesterday maybe he would have been ready today."

"Nice catch, Roscoe," Clancy said as he rode up. "Let me know the next time you feel lucky and I'll be ready for it."

Roscoe smiled.

"Well," he said, "we stand second."

Clancy nodded and got down to loosen his cinches.

"I'll be ready tomorrow," Clancy said, "and we'll take a first and we'll stand pretty high in the totals for the go-round money."

"Yeah," Roscoe said, "if we get good tomorrow we'll have a pretty fair average."

Old Clancy's all right, Roscoe decided; there's a lot worse heelers a man could be teamed up with. He's all right.

They drove into town together that night and had dinner. Roscoe was in high spirits. The next day, the last of the show, Roscoe caught their steer right at the handicap line and Clancy heeled perfectly. The crowd cheered as their near-record time was announced.

The winners were announced, and when the show was over Roscoe joined them in "the crying room" where they were paid their prize money. Roscoe drew his share of the go-round and day money for roping and his pay for judging and answered some questions from the younger riders.

"What could I have done different?" Carl Holt asked him.

"Not much, Carl, after you got that bad start. If I was you I'd study at bringing them out. I forgive a man a lot if he starts his horse strong. Look at the way Jerry Hunt scores a bronc and then how he spurs."

"Yeah," young Carl said, "he really rides them. With me it's just an ass and saddle fight."

"You could ride them as well as he does if you had the time at it he has," Roscoe said. "Jerry's ridden a lot of broncs and he's doing it all the time, not just once or twice a year. Cock your spurs into them and don't pull them out—drag them out."

Another rider wanted to know why he had not scored higher, and Roscoe explained that while he had spurred well with one foot it had looked like he was not using the other one much. The rider went away shaking his head.

"What the hell, Roscoe," Perry said as he came over to him, "why did you give Barney so much? He wasn't ever ahead of that Chico horse."

"Well," Roscoe said, "he was riding him like he was ahead of him. If he had ever weakened he would have gone off, but he just kept on riding. If that horse had of had sense enough to get out from under him he'd have been sitting on nothing, you're dead right. But I figured he was riding pretty good being so far behind the way he was."

Perry smiled at him.

"Let's go get us a drink," Perry said.

In the bar they met other contestants, and Hank Bartlett, the stock contractor who had supplied the bucking horses.

"You ought to chicken about half those goats, Hank," Roscoe said with a smile. "They're losing their pep."

"Hell, Roscoe," Hank said, "I'd like to but what they pay here for those horses doesn't leave a man enough to go out and buy good ones."

"It won't cost you any more to feed and haul good buckers than it does those skates," Roscoe said.

"Well," Hank said, "if I get this show next year maybe I'll bring some better stock, but I'll tell you one thing, if I do I'm going to get the whole show. I'm going to put my own pickup men in there, too. Those boys today, did you see the way they boxed those broncs before the whistle? That makes them look bad because they quit before the whistle."

"Yeah," Roscoe said, "they were kind of previous, but you got to remember, this ain't Cheyenne or Pendleton."

"No," Hank said, "but they want you to give them horses that the big shows would get and they won't pay for that kind of stock."

"I know," Roscoe said.

"Another thing, Roscoe, those boys didn't jerk loose the flank cinches when they picked up the riders. You know it doesn't do a bucking horse any good to run around half an hour with a tight flank cinch."

"Yeah," Roscoe said.

"No, sir," Hank went on, "if they want good stock they've got to pay for it and handle them right."

Roscoe moved down the bar, thinking: Nobody's satisfied. Everybody's got a beef. It's a helluva game.

But, he mused, it's a holdout for people like me. It's about the last place you see young men taking these things seriously and they've got to be encouraged. They can't learn it from a book.

Clancy turned from the bar to face him, growling, "Reno and then Winnemucca, eh, Roscoe?"

Roscoe nodded, "Reno and Winnemucca."

"Stay lucky," Clancy said.

"Do my best to," Roscoe said.

Chapter 12

IN 1926, just after Roscoe's forty-second birthday, he found himself back in northern Arizona working for the Bartons on the huge VB ranch. Buck Hastings bossed the crew and John Barton, Sr., still occupied the driver's seat of the Barton Land and Cattle Company. Buck had not yet given up his dreams in favor of the bottle and John Senior had not forsaken his empire in the mountains for a senatorial seat in Washington.

<Things were different before Buck jumped in the jug and John Senior went away. Not that I got anything against Jack Hastings or John Junior. It's just that things were different all the way around. Old Carter Henkle is about all that hasn't changed. Carter's still there.>

Carter Henkle had been the bookkeeper for the Barton Land and Cattle Company when Roscoe had gone on their payroll for the first time in 1903. It was Carter that Roscoe always saw first when he drifted back to Flagstaff looking for a job. Steve Barton had died and John Barton, Sr., had taken his place in the paneled office, and now John Junior sat in the big calfskin-covered swivel chair, but Carter Henkle still perched on his high stool behind the window marked "Cashier."

There was always the comfortable weight of the mellow

twenty-dollar gold pieces, the bulk of the silver dollars, and the crispness of the green bills which Carter had pushed toward him through that window over the years. Carter's eyes always smiled behind the distorting lenses of his thick glasses, and his voice was soft and considerate when he swung the thick pay ledger around to explain to Roscoe what the thin graceful figures on the blue-lined page added up to so far as Roscoe's financial standing with the company was concerned.

Carter would check the figures and explain them to Roscoe and ask, "Would you like to draw some?"

"How much trouble you think I can get into on twenty bucks?" was Roscoe's traditional question.

"About all you can handle," Carter would say. "How would you like it?"

"Any way it comes."

The ritual of speaking to the boss would follow. With old Steve, Roscoe had stood, as a kid should, with his hat held in front of his belt buckle, curling the brim tight with both hands. With John Senior he sat down and answered questions about range conditions; and with John Junior he talked about times past when John Junior had been a boy.

". . . and the time you took the latigo to me for changing the labels on the cinnamon and red pepper," young John would remember.

"Hottest damn pie I ever laid a lip over," Roscoe would say, smiling.

"Hottest tail end I ever had, too."

And then Roscoe would make his way out to the street for the traditional first couple of drinks with the rest of the crew. Their hangout was a small speakeasy off the main street which was known simply as "Black's," which had been their favorite saloon before Prohibition and still was, even with the windows boarded up. Billy Black, the owner, was usually to be found behind the warm dark wood of the bar smiling welcome in a dazzling display of gold teeth as he methodically polished the glasses.

"Come in, boys," he called. "Come in and have a touch."

He was a chubby red-faced man who knew the psychology of the kind of men who rode for the VB and treated them with the respect that their work warranted even when their conduct did not. Steadily twisting the already gleaming glass around the soft cloth, he welcomed them with his nicely turned demeanor, which was neither overbearing nor servile but a happy combination of good fellowship and admiration.

"It's good to see you. Been a long time," Billy always said, even if they had been in the day before. But this was not hypocrisy on his part. He was glad to see them, glad that they sought him out, happy to sell them drinks and to drink with them. He enjoyed the company of these men who got into town so seldom. He had ridden after cattle as a young man and had never forgotten those aspects of the work that he wanted to remember.

Billy bought every third drink and he saw to it that none of the VB boys left without having one last free one. This last drink was important because it proved Billy's good faith and hospitality. It could not possibly be construed as a come-on to encourage you to drink more and spend more, because you were leaving, and once you had accepted it you *had* to leave. He usually bought the first drink when the crew walked in.

"Have a touch," he said, "make yourselves to home. In Black's anything goes. Anything but me and the mirror."

They would drink for a while and then scatter to make various purchases of clothing, gear, or tobacco. Once they had safely cached their bundles they would meet again at Black's and drink until someone suggested eating.

"Alright," Buck Hastings would say, "anybody that wants to go on riding for the VB be by the store at four in the morning to go back."

Then the men were on their own. If they intended to go back to the ranch they would show up in the morning or be collected at the jail for the long trip out to the ranch.

<One time we were pretty short-handed and me and Buck were in Black's talking it over. This funny-looking

gink came up and hit Buck up for a job. "You done this work?" Buck asks him. "Oh, sure," the fellow says. But he doesn't look or act like it and it turned out he didn't have a outfit. Well, we were so hard up we'd take any kind of a warm body we could prop up in a gate so Buck tells him to meet us in the morning and we'd rustle up a outfit some way.

So me and Buck go on the town. Every now and again we'd notice this stranger in the joints we were touring. He'd smile and start trying to talk to us but hell, we didn't want to have him on our ear so we'd move on. He dogged us all night, and when we showed up at the truck in the morning there he was. Buck says, "I was hoping he'd get mad and blow." But there he was, bright as a button, and all the rest of us sicker than snakes and broker than the Ten Commandments.

We wait a while to see who's coming and who's in jail, and this guy is exercising his talking talents all along. Me and Buck sit down and try to get steady, and he talks on eighteen ounces to the pound. Pretty soon Buck he says, "Where the hell are the rest of the drunks!" This old boy chimes right in and says, "Yes sir, Mr. Hastings, that's something else you'll like about me. I don't touch spirits."

Well, we weren't paying too much attention; matter of fact, we were trying to shut out his noise. But that "Mr. Hastings" got our attention in spite of us. "No spirits?" Buck said like he thought the guy meant ghosts. "None," the fellow says, "I've never had a drink in my life." Well, old Buck he looks at him like this was the first time he ever saw such a thing and he says, "I just guess you better stick in town then. If you don't drink you couldn't stand it out where we're going!">

In 1926 they were not short-handed. In fact the VB was as well staffed, stocked, and operated as it had ever been. In addition to Buck and Roscoe, there was Dink Roberts. Dink, the lithe, wiry redhead who made a joke out of everything. There was Skip Green, a tall, slim Texan who seemed unable to drawl out any statement without gesturing with his long hands.

Skip contrasted with Dink in more than just physical aspects. Where Dink spoke rapidly and often, Skip contented himself with the briefest possible comments. As Dink chattered Skip would tip one corner of his extrawide mouth and nod or say, "You bet." His finely textured, flax-colored hair and faded blue eyes gave him a Scandinavian appearance.

Big Ben Larkin was working for the VB at that time. Ben was a simple-minded, huge man with a bushy head of coarse black hair. He believed in Buck Hastings completely and devoted all his mind and strength to carrying out Buck's wishes. He had considerable skill at handling animals and was one of the best horseshoers Roscoe had ever known. Ben kept his own string shod so well that he put the other men to shame, and often when the crew found themselves with a free afternoon Big Ben would go to the corrals and examine Buck's horses to see if they needed attention.

<Ben would get three or four ponies tied to the corral fence and just walk right down them resetting shoes faster and better than I ever saw it done. I hated horseshoeing. Hardest work I know. Ben never raised a sweat.

One time me and Dink saw old Ben working away and Dink thought we would have a little fun. He had a big roan horse in his string named Goober that was pure hell to shoe. I had helped Dink with that Goober and I knew. We had to throw him and tie all four legs. Then we'd run a pole between his legs, and while a man lifted up on each end of the pole Dink would get astride of it and go to nailing. Anyway, that was one mean horse to shoe.

So, like I say, Dink takes the big notion to slip Goober into Ben's string while he wasn't looking. We went to the corrals and I got old Ben to talking while Dink ropes out the big roan. When Dink had the pony tied at the end of Ben's line we went up to the bunkhouse and sat by the door to watch. Ben worked his way down toward that end of the line and you can see old Goober is getting the idea of what's about to commence to take place. He starts switching his hind end nervous like and looking over his shoulder and blowing big rolling snorts. Ben doesn't pay any heed. He just moves along steady.

About the time Ben gets to Goober little Dink is ready to split. He's slapping his leg and elbowing me and grinning like a skunk in a cabbage patch. I was about half holding my breath, too, because I figured that Goober horse would kick Ben right into the middle of next June. I was sure wrong.

Big old Ben gets to the roan and picked up a hind foot right off. Goober thought he was going to have something to say to that and he gave a great big jerk that would have pulled anybody else right off the ground. Right about then, when a man with any sense at all would have turned loose and run, Ben, who had a death grip on him and never lost hold, just jerks right back at him. He straightened that Goober's hind leg out with one pull so it stuck straight out behind. Dink and I heard the hip pop. Ben shakes it once or twice and tells him to mind.

Goober swings his head around to see what's happening to him, and you never saw such a surprised horse in all your life. Ben got that shoe set and clenched before he knew what was going on. Goober tested him again and got the same treatment, so he just settled down to think it over and pretty quick Ben was all done. Dink was sure amazed. A couple of months later little old Dink goes to reset those shoes thinking he can bluff Goober and came near getting killed, so we went back to throwing him.>

Monty Gerard was another member of the crew. He was a graceful man with the light hands and fine balance which spell the difference between riding on a horse and riding with one. When an exceptional colt showed up, Buck saw to it that as soon as the basic training was completed the colt was turned over to Monty who, with patience and firmness, soon had the young horse flexing and coming back on its hocks.

Monty was one of the few men Roscoe had ever known who received mail. Not just advertising from bootmakers, but real letters which had been written and addressed by hand. Where the letters came from or what they said Roscoe never learned because Monty never talked about himself. He would receive them without any show of emotion on his sharp-featured face, and as far as Roscoe knew he never answered them. When the fall work was finished Monty quit and Roscoe never heard of him again.

Joe Marky worked for the Bartons during part of 1926. He spent the rest of that year and the three following ones in the state penitentiary serving a sentence for robbery. Joe was a man with a problem. He was a good hand, a hard-working, good-natured man who was an asset to any crew. As long as he stayed away from town he was all right, but when he felt pavement beneath his feet he lost control of himself and indulged in excesses which society has seen fit to forbid. As a result he became familiar with the interiors of several cowtown jails.

Joe was a big, rough man with an ugly but amiable face who loved to drink and fight and raise hell in general. He did not fight because he was angry. To him battling was a means of self-expression. He went at it the way most men play games or exercise. Joe would leave a meal, a woman, or a horse race if offered the chance to fight.

Buck Hastings got Joe paroled out of the County Jail to come to work on the VB with the stipulation that Joe be kept out on the ranch for the duration of his sentence and that his wages be turned over to the madam who had signed a complaint charging Joe with demolishing the interior of her establishment. The brawl had been an eminently satisfactory one from Joe's point of view and well worth the price, but he was glad to get out of jail. It all started when someone told Joe that the house in question boasted a new bouncer who was reputed to be a pretty tough customer. "Good," Joe said, "let's go see just how tough he is." The bouncer turned out to be not quite tough enough.

Once Buck had secured his release and brought him out to the ranch, Joe was safe. He never quarreled and seemed to approach hard work with the same enthusiasm he exhibited going into a good scrap. Roscoe caught Joe studying Big Ben Larkin speculatively as the simple cow-

boy performed a feat of strength. Joe looked up at Roscoe
quickly and grinned, knowing that his thoughts were
apparent. "I'll just bet," Joe said, "that that Ben there
could give a man a awful tussle if he was to set his mind
to it." But that was as far as it ever went, and Joe gave
vent to his energy working. He stayed at headquarters
when the crew went to town, and Buck issued orders that
no whiskey could be brought back to the ranch. Joe's hair
grew down over his shirt collar, and Roscoe offered to
tie it up in a bun with meat string, Navajo fashion.

This was the nucleus of the crew that year. Extra men
were hired at certain times for special jobs which would
require more help. When they were getting ready to brand,
Buck went over the Bartons' books with Carter Henkle,
the bookkeeper, and got the names of cowboys who
owed the company for overdrawn wages. He scoured
the town with this list and picked up as many of them
as he could find. For the most part they were a pitiable
collection, having been interrupted in the middle of ex-
tended sprees.

<They were pretty sad, shaky and rum-dum. But once
they dried out they got over it and seemed sort of glad
to be along. That year Buck shanghaied old Cherokee
Brown and Mac McFadden and two or three others. We
put them at the fires ear marking and such where they
wouldn't have to work too hard. What hurt them most
was on the big circles. They had been a while away from
saddle work, and that Buck Hastings was no man to travel
with if you didn't want to lose your gut fat. He took out
early at a high lope and covered lots of ground.

We had some kid from the East out there for a while,
but he didn't last long. He stumbled around about as long
as he could stand it and then made up some phony excuse
about how he had to go home. We were all glad to see
him go. Old Buck made one of the longest speeches I
ever heard him get himself from around when we took
the kid to the depot. We knocked back a few fast ones
while he was drawing his money and Buck was getting

ornery when the kid came down and we took him to the
train. Buck had hold of his suitcase so the kid couldn't
get away. He said:

"Yeah, you go on home now. Go back and tell everybody you see what it was like and tell them to stay away.
But you won't. From now till you're a old man you'll sit
around telling everybody about when you were a cowboy
out West. You've been out in the world and now you
can go home and lean on your name for the rest of your
life. Your dead kin will carry you. Pretty quick you'll
forget how bad you thought it all was. You'll build up the
good you remember about it, and when you run out of
good to remember you'll make up some and if you keep
it up long enough you'll come to believe the crap you
made up. You'll get to where you won't be able to tell
what was real and what you made up or read in a book
or saw in a movie written by some other asshole who
didn't know either.

"You think we been hard on you, but you're wrong.
That's how life is out there. If the boys didn't mother up
to you all the way it was because they had good reasons
not to. A green hand on a outfit is a real pain in the ass.
He's worse. He's just plain dangerous. You stumble along
causing a lot of extra work and the boys are bound to
get ringy. But when you pull some dumb stunt like you
did spooking those ponies in the corral, getting two men
run down, they get pure mad. Leave a gate open and it
usually means a day's work to do over; stompede the
remuda and it could mean we'll be patting one of the
boys in the face with a spade.

"Sure, I've been boozing while you were up getting
paid off. But this is more than just whiskey talking. I'm
trying to tell you something so as you won't forget. Something you need to know. But, hell, maybe you don't need
to. You grew up getting all the sleep you wanted, resting
when you got tired and quitting when you got hurt.
You've got someplace to go back to. We don't. Not that
we want to. We were born into this and we'd feel strange
living any other way. Nobody's making us stay here. It's
not like we were in the army. We could all quit and go

to work in town but we won't and if you have to ask why, you'll never know.

"But there's a lot of other things you'll never know, too. You'll never know what we get out of doing something that tests a man's guts and doing it well. You may make a lot of money and be proud of your money, but that's different from being proud of yourself.

"We've got a lot of holes in us. Me and all the men on that crew. We'll never amount to a damn and likely we'll all die broke. We're easy to fault. But I'll tell you this: there isn't one I can't count on. They may look like dumb, dirty hillbillies to the likes of you, but they'll go out alone and get a job done knowing that they won't get thanked or paid extra for it. Maybe nobody would even know he did the job or if it was tough or if he hurt doing it. We could all soldier on the job. Easy. There's nobody out there checking on us while we're strangling in the dust, or sleeping in the rain, or freezing in the snow. We could dog it. But we don't and, like I said, if you have to ask why you'll never know.

"Hell. I'm running off at the mouth like a damn fool. I can't seem to get said what I want to. Like as not it makes no difference. I think I'll go across the street and finish off this drunk I've started. But remember this: I'll be there when the boys roll out in the morning. I'll feel like hell, but I'll be there. I'm not sure I know just what that proves, but you think on it while you're heading home.">

Chapter 13

IT WAS SOON after this that a natural phenomenon occurred on the VB which Roscoe never forgot. A strong west wind came up one evening and blew hard and steadily for six days. Nothing like it had ever been experienced in that part of the country. During the spring and fall windy days were expected, then the wind always died down at night to rise again with the sun.

But this was different. There was no relief at night. The wind roared around the bunkhouse twenty-fours a day rattling the windows, blasting sand against the glass, and testing the timbers with mighty gusts. The cattle drifted east with the wind until they piled up against fences where they stood stupidly bawling in a steady chorus which could not be heard over the noise of the gale. The sky was dark for days with dirt and debris. The men rode muffled with bandannas and scarves, vainly trying to shove the cattle down the fences to gates so that they would not pile up on each other and die. Buck managed to get to the highway and into town in search of extra help.

<It seemed like it was going to last forever. Like we were in some special kind of hell for cowboys. It was so damn steady. Pushing at you, pulling at you. Your head hurt from having your hat jammed down so hard. You couldn't smoke. You couldn't hardly breathe. We rode day and night trying to keep those cattle from ganging up. They walked right through some stout fences. We were trying to get them into the hills where there was timber and some shelter. I'll tell you, it was miserable.>

One of the men that Buck managed to find in town was Doc James. Doc was far from being anxious to come out and help, but Buck reminded him of his long-standing debt to the company, and with the promise that the entire amount would be taken off the books he threw his saddle and bedroll in the truck and came back with Buck. As it happened, he only put in three days of work before the big blow slacked off and then quit entirely as inexplicably as it had begun.

The men were exhausted and tense. The work had been enough to leave them drained, but the constant irritation of the wind had nibbled at their nerves, leaving them exposed and sensitive. They growled at each other and cursed their horses, the cattle, and the country. For days after the windstorm subsided there was none of the customary conversation in the bunkhouse.

Joe Marky was nursing a badly swollen hand which he had injured during the storm. Joe had found a band of cows which stubbornly refused to leave the comparative shelter of an arroyo to be driven to a gate which would let them up into the tree-covered foothills. He shouted himself sore-throated, kicked, crowded, and lashed with his rope, but the cows simply closed their eyes against the blows and bawled hoarsely. After what seemed hours of this struggle, Joe took down his hobbles and forced his way through the cattle, beating right and left with the buckle end of the heavy strap. Horns smashed against his legs and bruised him through the thick chaps.

Then his weary horse stumbled and fell in the midst of the surging animals. Joe managed to remount, and as he was turning back for another attack the cattle suddenly decided to move on for no apparent reason. They shuffled docilely out into the blast and let Joe work them out of the gate. Hours later Joe found his way back to the corrals at headquarters and swung stiffly out of the saddle. He was crouching downwind from his horse trying to untie the latigo when a sudden gust slammed against the pony, causing it to stagger. The horse stepped down hard on Joe's foot and for a moment fought for balance. The iron-shod hoof bore down on Joe's foot. Joe jerked at the reins and sent the horse back on its haunches.

The cowboy struck out blindly with all the force behind his heavy shoulders and smashed his fist into the metal bit. The sudden stabbing pain cleared his head, and he realized that it was not the horse that he struck out at and cursed but the wind, the steady, driving, maddening wind. Bruised and sore, he unsaddled the horse and stumbled toward the lights of the cookhouse.

Big Ben Larkin had torn a deep trough of flesh out of his right leg when some wind-driven cows had forced his horse against a barbed-wire fence and shoved him along against the wire for several feet. Monty Gerard's soft gray eyes were swollen nearly shut by a gust which had blasted a hatful of fine sand into his face. Some of the sand was still under the inflamed puffs of flesh which were his eyelids.

Roscoe had almost torn an ear off against the rough bark of a juniper limb as he dashed through the dark to head off some running steers. Buck had half a roll of adhesive tape wound around his right hand which he had rope-burned to the bone. Little Dink Roberts was for once without a wisecrack, and he had no energy for pranks. One of his front teeth had been knocked out and his lips looked like livid welts. Opening the heavy corral gate one morning, the wind had seized it and slammed it against his face. There was not a man among them who was not battered and sore. The storm had honed the triggers of their tempers.

Perhaps that was why Roscoe was so irritated by Doc James the night that he aired his theories. Doc was a stocky man with a square face, deeply cleft chin, and intense dark eyes. He was known as Doc because he professed to be knowledgeable in the field of veterinary medicine. The story had it that he had practiced as a vet in another state until he had been informed by the authorities that a formal education and license were required.

"Ontogeny recapitulates phylogeny," Doc was fond of saying, and most of the hands were impressed. Roscoe was not.

With the passing of the storm, the men went to work moving the cattle back to their normal ranges. The hills had to be searched and the mixed herds segregated, fences had to be repaired and dead cattle skinned. The long days were busy, and the weary hands wasted little time getting into their beds at night.

One evening after supper the crew were gathered in the bunkhouse. Roscoe lay on top of his bedroll fully clothed even to his star-roweled spurs. He stretched and groaned as he drew painful kinks out of his muscles. Dink and Big Ben were talking on the other side of the long narrow room.

"What did you do then?" Dink asked through his puffed lips.

"Do?" Ben said. "Hell! Nothing I could do. That old cow threw her tail up over her back and quit the country She's still running for all I know."

"What do you pack that lass rope on your saddle for?" Dink wanted to know.

"Never had no time to think on roping her," Ben grumbled. "Like I said, figured she was away down lower."

"That's the trouble with fellows like you," Dink said. "Think too much. That's what comes of . . ."

Roscoe stopped listening. Tomorrow was going to be another long hard day. He stretched again. If I could raise the strength to jack my yams out of these boots I'd go to bed, he was thinking, but he lay still. Buck Hastings appeared beside the cot looking down at Roscoe and grinning.

"You look like you were sent for and couldn't come," he said quietly.

Roscoe swung his legs over the edge of the cot and sat up. "That goddamn saddle of mine sure worked on my pistol pockets today. I'm waiting to see if it starts to eat both ways before I burn it up. It's been working on my butt like it was meat hungry, but none of my ponies is sorebacked yet."

A gust of wind rattled at the door to the bunkhouse like a dog asking to be let in, and all the men in the room turned nervously, waiting to see if the gale was starting up again. Buck laughed with an artificial cackle. "Come right in," he said loudly.

The gust passed and the men relaxed a little.

"Reminds me of when I was a kid," Buck said, addressing the silent room in general, "working over in New Mexico. Wind blew like hell the first day I went out with this old boy. Over there it's all wind and no water. The rain is pure wind and the wind is pure sand. I asked this old boy, 'The wind blow like this all the time?' He says, 'Hell, no. Sometimes it comes from the south.'"

A few of the men smiled, but no one laughed and Buck

sat down on the bunk beside Roscoe as the tension in the room relaxed and the hum of conversation began again.

Doc James came across the room toward them in an easy rolling gait which made the chunky man look like a deep-water sailor.

"When you aim to go to town, Hastings?" he demanded.

Buck tilted his ugly battered face up to look straight into Doc's intent stare. "Hadn't thought about it, Doc," he said. "Why?"

"Well, there's some of us that want to go in. We came to help you out of a bind and we figure things are about back to normal. You can get along without us."

Buck twisted his mouth into a grin.

"Yes," he said, "if the regular crew would put in twice as many hours horseback as they are now, I reckon we could do without you well enough, but I think you better stay awhile. Leastways till I get it figured out how I'm going to pack their grub out to them so they won't have to waste time riding in to eat."

Doc made a sour face. "Your troubles touch me deeply," he said, "but I've had enough of this and there are several others who think as I do so I would advise you to begin making plans for a trip to town. We feel that we have discharged whatever obligations we may have been under as far as the Bartons are concerned."

"Well, Doc," Buck said, "that may be. But I'm calling this dance and I'll let you know when it's time to stop."

Buck rose from the bunk and went out the door. Roscoe looked through the greasy window over his bed and watched him turn toward the dimly lit cook shack. The room had grown unnaturally quiet. Doc's broad, short-coupled back was turned to Roscoe but he heard his querulous voice say, "And what would you do if we went out on strike?"

Doc turned slowly, taking in the entire room. He was smiling with a sour grin.

"You heard him, boys," he continued. "We've got nothing to say about it. We go on this way until he decides to ease off. I for one have had a bellyful of working myself half to death for the Bartons' benefit."

"Come off it, Doc," Roscoe said. "You know it's got to be done."

Doc turned toward Roscoe.

"Perhaps it does, Roscoe, but have you stopped to think about the number of hours a day we have been putting in? Has anyone said anything to you about paying overtime? I think not. They'll pay you just what they feel like, and that will be damn near the same as they paid you ten years ago. Every day that much money buys less and every day you grow older. Unless you do something about it now you will wake up one day too old to do the work and with nothing to show for the years you have struggled as we are now."

"Hell, Doc," little Dink piped up. "I'll never feel no older than right now. Went out to pee a while back and had to lean against a fence post before I could muster up the gut muscles to squeeze the old bladder."

"Go ahead and joke if you want to," Doc said hotly. "But the time for joking is already past."

He had the attention of all the men in the bunkhouse and he hurried into his spiel which many of them had heard before. He used his hands dramatically as he talked, standing with his short legs spread and thrusting out his square jaw.

"This is 1926, damn it. The way we are working and living, the way we are paid and fed, you'd think it was fifty years ago. Maybe a lot of you don't know it, you've been out in the hills so long, but times have changed. You can get a job in town for three times what they pay you out here. Easier work and more money."

"Maybe we like it out here," Joe Marky said evenly, opening and closing his swollen fist.

Doc twitched his head toward Joe and nodded.

"Fine," he said. "That's fine, but is that any reason why you should be taken advantage of? Why shouldn't you try to make the life a little pleasanter, the work a bit more lucrative?"

Joe simply stared at him from where he sat on a horse-shoe keg beside the potbellied stove. His broad shoulders were hunched as if against the wind and he cradled his injured hand in his lap.

"Loo-cra-tive," Dink repeated. "I guess you got me there, Doc. Shuffle and deal again."

Doc shot him a scornful look and went on talking. He was a man who could not disagree without becoming disagreeable. Roscoe had heard this union argument before from Doc and it never failed to make him uncomfortable. He distrusted the theory but could not articulate his reasons. Wages and hours were foreign to his thinking. Some times of the year you worked extra hard and others you simply drifted through.

"When I work for a man," Roscoe said, "I always give him a little more than he's paying for. That way I'm not beholden to him for the job. I don't like to owe anybody."

The others in the room talked back to Doc as they warmed to the subject. Monty Gerard maintained his customary silence, but he nodded occasionally when Dink turned to him for support. Big Ben Larkin squatted on his boot heels beside the stove like an immense gaping tree toad, turning his head from speaker to speaker. No one asked his opinion, but he nodded or shook his head in agreement when one of the regular hands made a point.

Roscoe had tried to make an occasional point, but quick-witted Doc had blunted and turned aside his protests, parrying and thrusting with a verbal facility far beyond Roscoe.

As the men began to yawn and turn to their beds, the argument tapered off and Doc had the last word. Roscoe stripped down to his underwear and slid between his blankets. He was tired and his body ached but he had trouble going to sleep. He wished that he could think of something to say that would turn Doc off, but he could not.

Chapter 14

THE ROAD, if you could call it one, was rutted so deep that Roscoe's pickup and trailer dragged occasionally on the center ridge. The ruts were obviously not caused by any great use because there was grass growing in the tracks. Roscoe bumped and scraped along, praying that he would not crack the pan or knock out the rear end. It had been a lean year and there was no money in the till for an expensive repair job.

The country was typical of northern Nevada: low hills studded with pinion pine, green dots against the red earth making the hills look like big hams with cloves stuck in them. The road ducked around these hills and steadily worked its way higher and higher toward the mountains. The mountains behind the hills were dark green and, this being the fall of the year, they had streaks of golden aspen groves across their faces.

On and on Roscoe drove, and the country did not change. Roscoe passed a string of steers trotting in single file, their heads swaying and their lean flanks flapping in the opposite direction from the loose hide hanging from their briskets. They jogged along rhythmically, floppily, looking as though they were out of step with themselves. For no good reason they decided to cross in front of Roscoe as he had half expected that they might.

He slowed and stopped. The steers seemed in poor flesh to be going into the winter. Roscoe lit a cigarette as he waited, and then he looked back to the desert floor which he had climbed from after leaving the highway. The land below was gaunt and barren as a sun-bleached skeleton. A grim and bitter country, dun-colored and speckled with metallic green brush. He could make out two or three bands of sheep clustered like lice on the plain. God help that Indian, he was thinking, if this turns out to be a wild-goose chase.

The Indian, a majestic specimen with his hair tied up in back with meat string, had told Roscoe that the year before he had been back into this country gathering pinion nuts and had seen any number of wild horses. Roscoe questioned the big fellow as long as he could stand the smell of wet wool that hung about him and decided that even if you took his figures and split them in half, which is what you always had to do, there would still be plenty of broomtails in these hills. Enough anyway to make a hunt worth the try. The poke being empty as it was, he had loaded old Soldier in the trailer and here he was.

But he would have to be quick. It could snow any time now at this altitude. The last steer crossed, and Roscoe started up grade. He chuckled at the memory of the serious face of the Navajo as he had spun his obviously exaggerated tale about the herds of mustangs. I guess, Roscoe mused, that it's because they want to tell you what you want to hear. You're looking for horses, they come up with thousands of them. You don't want to have to haul them far, so they halve the distance. I've gone damn near twice as far as he said already and I'm near to certain I've got a ways to go yet. Obliging bastards.

In town he had inquired and been told that a family named Reilly had a place up on top, and that was where he was headed. He would need help. Horse meat was worth six cents a pound, and with luck he should be able to truck out a thousand dollars' worth of the inbred mustangs before the snow came. All he had to do was corral them and then order the trucks from town.

On he went, bumping and scraping, trying now and then to ride the edge of the road. The trailer forced him to use his lower gears most of the time. He rounded a hill and looked out over a grass flat surrounded by big sugar pines. A stream wiggled across the flat, and beyond the stream, at the upper end of the meadow, was a cabin with a barn and corrals. Smoke curled from the chimney of the cabin.

Roscoe was busy checking where the horses could be held and loaded. He could almost feel the comfortable bulge of bills in his pocket as he slid the pickup into second gear and started toward the corrals. The stream was shallow and the road just ducked under it, so he went across. It had a good bottom and there was no trouble.

By the time he rattled up on the far side three shepherd dogs had come down from the cabin and herded him along, yapping at his tires. He pulled up by the corrals where he saw a man feeding some bulls and shut off the motor. He knew how strangers had to handle themselves around mountain people if they wanted to get any place with them. You don't ever want to hurry them, he was thinking, or act like there is anything strange about you being there even when you know there is.

He got out of the truck, and the three dogs came up stiff-legged and sniffing. Roscoe treated them just as he planned to treat their owners: as though there was nothing unusual about his being there or about their being where they were, either. They sniffed his legs and then turned their attention to the truck's tires. Moving unhurriedly, Roscoe went back to the trailer and climbed up to see how Soldier had made the trip. The big bay raised his handsome head and looked up at him inquiringly. Roscoe winked, patted the horse's glossy neck, and hopped down.

The man in the corral had glanced up when Roscoe arrived and then had turned back to his work. Hell, Roscoe thought, he acts like pickups pulling horse trailers cruised through here a hundred times a day. You can see that the road ends there at the cabin. Probably nothing been by here since the last migration of buffalo, but that guy turns away like he was tired of the traffic.

The dogs trailed him to the fence where he waited instead of climbing over as he would have done had he been nearer civilization. Get too forward with these folks, he was thinking, break a rule and you might just as well forget about the whole thing and go away. So he waited, leaning against the peeled pole fence while the man inside shook out clusters of rank meadow hay to the coarse bulls. The dogs sniffed and peed and scratched the ground.

Finally the man in the corral jammed his pitchfork into the top of the haystack, jumped down, and started toward Roscoe, who studied him covertly from beneath the brim of his hat. Roscoe was startled because for some reason he had not expected to see anyone young way back in the woods like this. Somehow this boy seemed out of place. He was tall, well built, and had a ruddy, well-scrubbed face which appealed to Roscoe. Still in his early twenties, Roscoe judged.

"Hello," Roscoe said, not sure of where he went from there but knowing that it would come to him.

The young man nodded, smiling. That makes it my turn again, Roscoe told himself.

"Nice-looking bunch of bulls," he said, tilting his head toward the scrubs, who were horning each other aside at the hayrack. The young man looked at Roscoe quickly and then turned to the bulls almost as if he wanted to make sure that he knew what animals this stranger could be referring to. The way he cocked an eyebrow at him told Roscoe that this fellow wasn't fooled a bit.

"Well," the young man said slowly as if he did not want to contradict Roscoe but knew that he was wrong as hell, "they aren't much for looks, but they're stout."

They were, too, Roscoe saw—long-backed and rough looking, about as typey as so many desert jackrabbits. Roscoe decided to try again.

"I guess," he said, "up here it doesn't matter so much what they look like so long as they cover the country— the country and the cows."

The boy smiled and turned again to watch the bulls feeding. Roscoe decided: This youngster knows which way the wind is blowing and he isn't going to be fooled into thinking something just because he might want to.

"Yeah," the boy said, "in this country the stock has got to rustle."

This, Roscoe knew, could go on all day so he came right out and said, "I hear there's some wild horses running up here." He watched the boy's face for any change of expression but there was none so he went on. "I thought I might make a try at running in a few while there's still weather left to truck them out."

The young man hesitated and then said slowly, "Yes. There are a couple of bands in the hills. My wife's dad used to catch some years back, but since he got hurt he gave it up."

He was gazing toward a ridge to the north, and Roscoe marked in his memory a strange rock formation.

"Well," Roscoe said, "maybe we could make a deal."

The boy nodded. "Have to talk to my father-in-law, but I've got a good idea he won't mind. The broomtails are a headache. Always busting fences and trying to run off our saddle stock."

They walked together toward the cabin of logs which seemed to blend into the pines around it as they swayed together above the roof like old women whispering scandal. The dogs ran ahead, and a woman in a blue dress appeared in the doorway of the little house with a pan of water held before her. She sloshed the water about and then tossed it out of the pan into the yard dust. For a moment she stood watching them approach and then vanished into the cabin.

A moment later an old man came to the door and watched as they walked toward him. He stayed watching as they crossed the yard and came to the doorway. My God but he's ancient, was the first thing Roscoe thought as he took in the stooped figure and wrinkled face. But as he got closer he realized that the man's back was bowed beyond the ordinary bend of time and the lined face was twisted into a grimace of pain. It was the face of a man who had suffered for so long that he wore a perpetual mask of agony which made him look older than his years.

"How are you?" Roscoe said to the old man, who shuffled backward, nodding and offering entrance to the house. Once inside and seated around an oilcloth-covered table, the young man offered introductions. His name was Bud Armstead, the girl was his wife, Patsy, and her father was Tim Reilly. He explained to the old man the purpose of Roscoe's visit.

"I've got a contact in Yearington," Roscoe said, "and I figured you might want a few of the pests off your range."

"They ain't good for nothing," old Tim said, straining the words through his teeth. "All runts and throwbacks."

"They're good for dog food," Roscoe said. "Worth maybe three, three and a half cents a pound."

"That much?" Tim said.

Roscoe had to look away as he lied about the value of horse meat, but when Tim seemed to accept his story he felt better. After all, he reasoned, the mustangs would all die of old age if it weren't for him.

"Yeah," Roscoe said. "That's what they're bringing in Yearington. Getting them there is another story."

The girl Patsy came to the table and placed chipped mugs of steaming fragrant coffee in front of each of them. Roscoe smiled his thanks and noticed that she was strikingly pretty and fresh. Lots of wavy hair, blue-gray eyes, and an oval face with dimples. Her figure was stocky and utilitarian, but she moved with grace. Women in the woods that Roscoe had seen were not usually so neat and feminine. She joined them at the table, flashing Roscoe a quick smile as he rose automatically.

"It seems a pity," she said. "They look so pretty running on the mountain."

"Yes," Roscoe said, "there's nothing freer and finer to see than a band of horses running loose. But most mustangs anymore don't look so good close up. Being in little bunches and breeding back, they're mostly deformed freaks."

"Years back," Tim said, "there was some corking good ones up here."

"Yes," Roscoe said, "I've run mustangs all over the country for a long, long time and I've seen my share of first-class horseflesh amongst them, but now they're runty. Nowadays they come so cow-hocked they can't run without knocking their legs together. Some have big heads like draft horses and legs no longer than Shetland ponies. They're potbellied and ewe-necked."

"If there was a good one," young Bud asked with an elaborate casualness which Roscoe caught, "would you try breaking him to ride?"

"Oh," Roscoe said, watching Patsy glance quickly at Bud, "a man might try. But the biggest part of the time you're sucking eggs unless you get a young one. Besides, horses are so cheap now it's not worth your time. Nowadays if you're good and mad at somebody you give them a horse. Darn few mustangs worth fooling with now. You can peddle the good kind for blood horses, though."

"Blood horses?" Bud asked.

"Yeah," Roscoe said. "There's an outfit down in Phoenix that uses them to make some kind of serum. They keep horses and give them some kind of infection. I don't know just how it works, but they take blood from these horses, a little at a time, and use it to make medicine. Tetanus shots or something."

"You get money for that kind?" Tim asked.

"A little," Roscoe said cautiously, "But that kind's got to be clean and healthy. No marks or sores."

The conversation went on, and gradually Roscoe felt that he had been accepted and that he was at least going to have a chance. Patsy shooed them all out of the kitchen so she could get supper ready, and they went down to unload Soldier.

Roscoe noticed that while old Tim was permanently stooped he seemed agile and able to move around without too much difficulty. On rare occasions he managed to twist his face into a distortion Roscoe assumed was a smile. The results were horrible but somehow encouraging to Roscoe simply in view of the fact that a man so afflicted could still muster a smile.

Both Tim and Bud expressed genuine admiration for Soldier when Roscoe backed the big horse out of the trailer. They turned him loose in a corral by himself where he promptly lay down to roll and rub in the dust. He rose and shook, blowing long rolling snorts. Roscoe hung a moral of oats on the bay's head while Bud filled the hayrack. While they waited for Soldier to finish his grain, they talked about the mustangs.

"We can use my old trap," Tim said. "I reckon it wants some patching up, but that's easy done."

"Where's it located?" Roscoe asked.

"Up on the tableland," Tim said, pointing toward a flat just below the rock formation Roscoe had noticed earlier. "I built it around the only living water up there, and the horses have been going in there to drink for years now."

Roscoe nodded as he studied the mountainside. Rough country, he was thinking, but no worse than a lot of places he had run horses in. If they could pick up a band down below and get it started up the draw below the tableland, the rest would be easy.

Patsy called them in to supper, and Roscoe ate hungrily. It was a good meal: little steaks cooked in a Dutch oven with rich brown gravy and big sourdough biscuits. Patsy kept the platter heaped high with the light crusty biscuits and smiled with approval as they disappeared.

"I can't seem to quit," Roscoe said.

Later Roscoe took his bedroll out of the pickup and carried it to the hay shed where he made his bed on the sweet-smelling meadow grass. But he did not sleep well. There were chickens roosting in the rafters, and three weaner pigs kept coming in to root around the dirt floor. Roscoe was restless, and he decided that the next night he would move his bed to the pickup and sleep in the back the way he usually did when he was on the road.

They rode up to the trap the next day, and Roscoe was impressed with the way old Tim was able to handle himself in the saddle. Humped over the horn, he moved along at a good clip. Roscoe examined the approach to the trap and decided that it was well set up. From the amount of sign along the draw, it was obvious that Tim was right, there had been a number of horses up and down the trail recently. They set to work reinforcing the wings leading into the trap and the fence around it. They worked all day and returned to the cabin for supper just before sundown.

"I wish we were better mounted," Bud said as they went over their plan. "None of our saddle horses are much for speed. You and that Soldier are going to have to turn the trick."

They went over their plan again. Roscoe was to work any of the wild bunches they could find along the base of the mountain to Bud, who would be at the entrance to the draw. Bud was to turn the herd up the canyon, and Tim would be hidden there. When they passed him, Tim would push them up into the trap and block the gate. It sounded simple. At Roscoe's suggestion they decided to tie three or four gentle horses inside the trap to help lure the mustangs in.

"When did you build that trap, Tim?" Roscoe asked.

"Years back," the old man said, "when I first homesteaded here. Spent lots of nights up there sitting in a hole with a rope tied to the gate. When a bunch came in to water I figured to jerk the gate shut on them."

The old man stopped and Roscoe waited. When he did not go on, Roscoe asked, "What kind of luck did you have?"

"All bad," Tim said, and the lines in his face deepened.

Roscoe waited, but Tim did not go on so Roscoe began to talk to cover up the uncomfortable silence. He described the season he had spent working farther south in Nevada with a partner who hazed mustangs with an airplane. Roscoe would wait near the trap, and when the pilot drove the horses near enough he would run them in horseback. He told about the days during World War I when he had run horses in Oregon. He recalled the old tales he had heard about how the Indians used to walk mustangs down afoot.

"They just packed some meal or jerky in a sack and kept after them," he said. "They'd always be there day and night and never gave the horses a chance to stop and feed or rest. Kept them moving till the herd got so tired and hungry they didn't much care, and then the Injuns could steer them into a trap."

He told about the smart studs he had seen bossing bands of horses and how, when he sensed danger, the

stud would sometimes charge right through the herd
scattering the mares so they could not be caught in a
bunch.

"Don't let anybody spin you a yarn about seeing a
broomtail stud 'lead' his bunch out of trouble. They don't
lead, they drive. One of the old mares gets in front and
he gets behind, biting and kicking, driving and turning
them. He might get in front when he doesn't know where
the trouble is apt to come from, like when they're going
to water, but just as quick as he figures out where the
danger is he gets behind and whips them up."

He talked compulsively for some time without really
knowing why he felt so uneasy. When he left he was too
tired to move his bed down to the pickup parked beside
the corral, so he stayed in the barn. It was the same as the
night before: chickens, pigs, and very little sleep. He went
over his plans. The next day or two should tell. One
good thing, he told himself, a bunch in this kind of country this late in the year are not likely to sell out and
quit their range. They may make a couple of good runs,
but they will circle. He finally dozed off and dreamed of
herds of running horses.

They rode out early the next day, circling down into
the greasewood and juniper flats on the other side of
the mountain. Tim hunched over his saddle horn and
jogged along tirelessly. Soldier was feeling fine and made
the other horses strain to keep up with his swinging stride.
They saw nothing that day, but the next day they found
fresh sign and on the third day they jumped a band of
thirty or forty head.

They flushed out of a thicket like a covey of quail. An
old crop-eared blue mare was in the lead, and a buckskin
stallion drove them toward the mountains. Once the stud
stopped and turned to look back at them. Roscoe waited
for Tim and Bud to catch up with him.

"They aren't spooked much," Roscoe said. "They
won't go far. We'll get a better look at them tomorrow."

But they did better than that. They found the horses
just above the entrance to the draw that led to the trap.
Tim and Bud took cover while Roscoe circled far below

the plateau. Soldier sensed the excitement and stretched out into a long rolling lope, shaking his head for more rein.

"Take it easy," Roscoe warned him, "you might just get your bellyful of running before we get done."

But it went off more smoothly than Roscoe had dared to hope. Once beyond the herd, he showed himself, and the mustangs turned back, skirting the edge of the flat. He let Soldier out and easily held his position on the outside and a little behind. Bud appeared at just the right instant, and the horses plunged into the ravine, thundering up toward the trap. Bud's horse played out quickly, and Roscoe sailed past him as he heard Tim whoop.

Soldier leaped up through the rocks and soon overtook Tim and passed him. He swept past a limping colt and came upon the buckskin stud just as he was driving the last mare through the narrow gap that marked the gate to the trap. Roscoe slid to a stop and threw himself out of the saddle to slide the poles across the opening. It was all over. The next few days were spent moving the mustangs down to the corrals a few at a time, mixed with the gentle horses. Roscoe was able to relax only after the last one was safely in the home corral. He leaned against the gate and studied the herd. They were fair, he was thinking, just fair. The full-grown horses would be lucky if they averaged eight hundred pounds apiece. The colts and yearlings might pay the freight bill. Roscoe watched the buckskin stud rushing from one side of the corral to the other, stopping occasionally to emit a high whistling snort. He had mean white-rimmed eyes and he carried his head low and outthrust like a snake. Crazy as a pet coon, Roscoe said to himself, and turned away.

Tim was hobbling up and down the fence, ducking and raising his head, looking over and under the poles. His lips moved silently. Roscoe watched the old man and realized that he was studying the stallion. Bud came down from the house and joined his father-in-law at the fence. They talked together without taking their eyes off the pacing buckskin, then Bud went back to the cabin. Roscoe followed a little later.

"How about some of that good coffee?" he said as he stepped through the door. Patsy was standing in front of the stove and Bud was seated at the table. From their expressions it was obvious that he had walked in on an argument but it was too late for him to do anything about it so Roscoe barged right in as though he had not noticed anything. Patsy gave him a mugful of coffee and turned her attention to a pot on the stove. Bud sat glowering at the floor.

"I'm not much at sums," Roscoe said, "so you're going to have to help me figure a fair split on this deal."

Bud did not look up.

"I've only got around two hundred bucks on me but I could give you that," Roscoe said.

Bud slowly shook his head.

"Well," Roscoe said, "you'll have to wait till I get the horses sold if you figure on more, but I think . . ."

Bud continued shaking his head. "We don't want money," he said in a low voice. "Just leave us that buckskin and we'll call it square."

Roscoe looked at him and opened his mouth but shut it again without saying anything. Patsy whirled away from the stove.

"Tell him!" she said angrily. "Tell him how crazy it is."

Roscoe was thinking that at best the stud would bring about thirty-five dollars. Here I am straining a gut to give him two hundred bucks and he wants to settle for that crowbait. I should give him the horse and leave before he comes to.

"If that's the way you want it," Roscoe said.

Patsy slammed a stove lid back in place, threw the lid lifter into the woodbox, and rushed out the door. Bud still did not look up. Roscoe rose.

"Don't mind her," Bud said quietly. "She'll simmer down."

"Maybe I best get down the mountain," Roscoe said, "and order the trucks."

"No," Bud said, "wait till morning. She'll be all right in a bit."

Roscoe left the cabin and started toward the corrals where he could see Tim watching the horses. It doesn't make sense, he was thinking. Patsy was at the edge of the yard throwing scratch to the chickens. She tossed the feed as if each handful were something she wanted to get rid of. Roscoe lowered his head and started by her.

"I'm sorry I blew up, Roscoe," she said, and Roscoe looked up.

She walked to his side and stood looking down toward the corrals.

"It's just that I don't want to see him hurt," she said, and Roscoe could not think of anything to say.

"Look at my father," she went on. "He's worse than Bud. You'd think he would know better. I don't want Bud all crippled up like that. I still wake up nights remembering when Dad was hurt. My mother was alive then. She brought him in the house all over blood and washed him off some and went for a doctor. I was little but I had to sit with him almost all night before they got back."

She paused and Roscoe found his voice.

"What happened?" he asked.

"He was breaking a horse. Somehow it got him down and stomped on him. Mom ran down waving her apron and drove it off. Nobody thought he could live through it, but he did."

Roscoe looked down the gentle slope to the corrals and the bent figure peering between the poles.

"I don't want that to happen to Bud," she said and paused. "Why are men such fools about horses?"

Roscoe tried to smile.

"I'm sorry I got mad," Patsy said. "I'm kind of upset. You see, I'm going to have a baby in the spring and . . ."

Her voice trailed off and Roscoe saw the tears well up in her eyes. She turned away and went toward the house. Roscoe stood for a moment looking after her and then started down to the corral.

"Did Bud ask you?" Tim wanted to know.

"About the stud?" Roscoe said. "Yeah."

"Good. Good," Tim said. "Ain't he a dandy?"

Roscoe looked at the stud to make sure that they were both talking about the same thing. The mustang had not improved. He was still a common little broomtail with a ratty look around his eyes and broken feet. But Roscoe had learned a long time ago that when it came to horses it was best to tell people what they wanted to hear no matter what you really thought. He examined the mustang, trying to find something good he could say about it.

"He looks like he'll pack a man a long way," was the best that he could come up with, and from the look Tim flashed at him he could tell that that was not enough.

Bud came down from the house and joined them at the fence.

"Can you cut him away from the bunch?" Bud asked.

"Sure," Roscoe said. "Why?"

"Well, as long as you're here to help I thought I might just try to ride him."

"Yeah," Tim said, "dab a loop on him and snub him up good. That's the idea."

Roscoe started to protest, to offer suggestions about starving the stud for a while to weaken him, or working him from the ground for a time before saddling him, but Bud was already going for his saddle. He went to the other pens and brought Soldier out, thinking: Maybe I can talk him out of taking the stud after he gets piled.

Roscoe tightened both cinches and rode Soldier into the pen with the mustangs as they fluttered to the far fence like so many chickens. When he got the gate to the loading pen open, he backed off and gradually worked in against the horses until he got them started through the gate. Each time the stallion tried to get through Roscoe jumped Soldier in and turned him back. Soldier marked the stud, and it did not take them long to work the herd into the pen away from him. Roscoe took his rope down. The stud was circling the corral now with his head up and his tail stretched straight out behind.

Roscoe debated as to whether he should catch him by the front feet and throw him or take him around the neck and choke him down. Maybe, he thought, I can break his goddamn neck. He waited for the stud to go by and then, giving the loop two quick turns, he jumped Soldier in, quartering on the stallion, and caught him neatly, jerking the loop tight just behind the ears. Soldier squatted and the stud came over backward. If he was any good, Roscoe thought, that would have killed him, but he's just like a bad rope that you can't break.

They tied the stallion to the big snubbing post and blindfolded him before putting on Bud's saddle. Bud mounted, and Roscoe removed the heavy cotton rope first and then got on Soldier and rode up to pull the blindfold off. For a moment the stud stood trembling, and then he exploded into action. After two jumps Roscoe saw that Bud was going off, and he pointed Soldier at the pitching horse. The big bay knew what was expected of him. He flattened his ears against his neck and dove at the stud, but he was too late.

Bud went off the far side just as Roscoe was reaching for the hackamore rein. Roscoe dallied the heavy rein around his saddle horn and jerked the stud away as Bud rolled against the fence, safe from the lashing hooves. Bud got quickly to his feet and came to help remove the saddle. Just then Roscoe looked over at the fence and saw Patsy standing beside her father. Her face was unnaturally white.

Supper was a strain. Old Tim mashed his beans, and there was little or no conversation. As soon as he could, Roscoe left the cabin and went to the corrals to take care of the last chores. Although he had finally managed to sleep well in the barn, he decided to move his bed to the pickup so that he could get a good early start down the mountain. It was a clear night and the moon was very nearly full. It was so bright that Roscoe did not sleep right away. When he did doze off the horses fighting woke him.

He lit a cigarette and lay there thinking about the buckskin. Old Tim wants that stud tamed. Why? It must have something to do with the bronc that broke him up. Bud wants the horse the way a kid wants a real locomotive without knowing what having one involves. Patsy, she knows. She's got sense enough for all of them but it isn't going to do her much good. And me? I'm going away from here.

But, he asked himself, is that going to be the end of it? Are you going to be able to give up wondering if that snaky sonofabitch has got to Bud or not?

With the last drag on the cigarette an idea came to him. He could just get up and open the gate to the stud's pen. The horse would be gone in the morning and he could take the blame for being careless with the latch. He could give them the two hundred and go. He was weighing the idea when he heard something over by the gate to the corral. He raised his head and looked over the edge of the truck bed. There in the bright moonlight was old Tim. He had his nightshirt tucked into his jeans, and he hobbled up to the gate and opened it. He swung the gate all the way open and looked in at the stallion.

"Go on, son," he muttered, "get gone."

The stud backed up, snorting. Tim left the gate open and limped back up toward the house. The stud whistled twice and backed into the farthest corner. Roscoe decided that he wanted to think this over, so he got up and closed the gate and got back in bed. Why did the old man want to turn the horse loose? Did he get to thinking it over and change his mind? If I let him go now, Roscoe thought, the old man will figure he did it. Some day it might come out and Bud would be sore as a boil.

The clouds sailed across the moon, and Roscoe lay thinking. When he heard the gate hinges creak he peeked over the edge of the truck bed again and saw Bud opening the gate. Bud looked at the stud for a long time, and the horse just backed away snorting.

"Go on before I change my mind," Bud said.

The stallion kept backing away, so Bud left the gate open and went up the path toward the house. Roscoe watched the horse, and the horse watched the gate, snorting and staying as far away from it as he could get. A half an hour later he was still just standing there. Roscoe got up and pulled on his jeans and boots. I'm going to have to run that son of a gun out of there, he thought. Then

he heard footsteps. It was Patsy with a big coat wrapped
around her nightgown. She stopped when she saw the
open gate.

"Hello," Roscoe said as gently as he could, but she
jumped just the same.

"What are you doing here?"

"Trying to sleep," Roscoe said, "but I'm not having
much luck."

"It looks like you saved me the trouble," she said,
nodding toward the open gate. "Thanks."

"Don't go thanking me," Roscoe said. "I don't suppose
you were aiming to turn that horse loose?"

She nodded.

"That seems to be the game we're playing tonight,"
Roscoe said. "Two other people, not to be naming names,
have snuck down here one at a time to do the same
thing."

Patsy stared at him for a moment and then smiled, and
the smile grew into a low laugh.

"You say both of them did?" she said.

"Yeah," Roscoe said. "I couldn't figure what got into
everybody."

"I thought Bud was just going to the john," she said
with a grin.

"No," Roscoe said, "he came down here. Your dad
was first. I closed the gate after he left. Then Bud came.
Now you."

"Why did you close the gate the first time?"

"I just wanted to see if you were all of the same mind,"
Roscoe said and started toward the corral to run out the
stud.

"Go to bed now," he said. "He'll be long gone by
morning."

Driving down toward the desert the next morning,
Roscoe passed another string of steers grazing their way
along from nowhere in particular toward nowhere special.
Or perhaps, he thought, that's the same bunch, still on
the go, not going away from anything or to anything, just
going. The lonely dawn light moved across the land below,

adding a hint of color to the drab plain. Roscoe drove slowly, letting his eyes stretch themselves, taking in the great distances ahead. He had a long way to go but was not in a hurry. No one was waiting for him.

PART

3

<He was quite a boy, old Skip. Somebody that didn't really know him might say he did everything the hard way. It looked like that sometimes, but that wasn't it. Take the way he had to catch a horse. Always stood them up in the corner and roped them. No matter if it was the only horse in the corral and it wanted to get caught Skip would get out his lass rope and dab a loop on it. I've seen him handle thousands of horses and he rope-broke them all whether they were wild or gentle. He'd take a bronco colt and tie a big cotton rope hard and fast so it couldn't choke high up on the colt's neck. He'd tie the other end to the bottom of a corral post. When he pitched his catch rope at the colt it would naturally spook and run. Skip would beller a big "Whoa!" just about the time the colt got to the end of the cotton rope and got jerked over backward. Didn't take long till he could throw ropes at that colt all day without it running off.

He never let one get broke to catch by hand. Never used a pail of oats or a moral to catch one. Didn't want a horse to look like it was raised a pet. Sometimes it didn't really make much sense, but that was his way. He had a way to do everything. If it was driving a staple or making bread, there was a way to do it and that was the way it got done. Like he figured that taking a shortcut or easier way was cheating, and he was never a man to cheat. I know the feeling. I'm some ways the same.>

Chapter 15

IT WAS the dry time of what had been a very dry year and Roscoe drove slowly down the narrow dirt road which led from the highway into the heart of the brush country of the Big Bend in Texas. The road twisted through an inferno of impenetrable undergrowth, and it was hot, hot, hot. Dust rose up through the floorboards of the car, and Roscoe wondered how the hell anybody, even Skip Green, could come to settle in such a forsaken place. They had told him at the rodeo that Skip had a place out here, "a starvation brushpile of a place," they called it, and Roscoe had set out to find his old friend.

Occasionally the road broke into clearings dotted with scrub oak trees and then plunged back into the jungle of brush. It was in one of the larger clearings that Roscoe found Skip's place: a low adobe house and barn with corrals made of twisted poles stood upright and lashed together with heavy smooth wire. Several small adobe sheds and outbuildings stood about baked by the scorching sun, casting deep purple shadows. Three horses and a small red mule in the corral hung their heads in the heat, and as the car turned toward the house a pack of multicolored shepherd dogs rushed out, barking hysterically. Roscoe slowed and stopped in the shade of an ancient oak just as the tall slim figure of a man appeared in the doorway of the house and shouted at the dogs. It was Skip all right. A good deal older, a shade leaner, but the same old Skip. Roscoe got out of the car as Skip stepped off the low-walled veranda. In an instant they were shaking hands.

*   *   *

They sat on the abbreviated veranda, which was shaded and cool. The dogs sprawled around their chairs, panting and at rest, but each of them seemed alert, as if at any moment they expected to be given a signal. As the two friends talked Skip would occasionally lean forward and squirt a stream of tobacco juice out over the adobe wall of the porch into the dust. A few streaks of brown down the inside of the low wall showed where he had sometimes misjudged. He was a lean, weatherbeaten man and everything about him seemed worn, from the faded jeans with frayed cuffs to the deeply lined hide on the back of his neck. His face was a study in fine lines and his long-fingered hands moved expressively as he talked. Roscoe was reminded of the old days on the VB and they reminisced together. Skip had a way of tipping up one corner of his wide mouth in a twisted grin and saying. "You bet," in agreement or for emphasis.

The sun gradually dipped behind the little house and the shade moved out toward the car. Several brown, yellow-legged chickens came to wallow and fluff themselves, bathing in the dust of the yard, and a wind devil danced crazily up the road. One of the blue and black dogs rose and came to rest its broad intelligent head on Skip's leg. Skip automatically dropped one long hand down to stroke the animal.

"Suppertime," he said and got to his feet.

Roscoe and the six dogs followed him around the corner of the house to a huge cauldron mounted on a neatly constructed brick base. With a long-handled ladle Skip scooped up portions of gray meat for each dog into tin plates which he distributed on the ground. Each time he bent to put down a plate he said a dog's name and that dog would come forward while the others waited tensely.

"I knock over an old doe for them now and again," Skip said.

They returned to the house, moving through the cluster of hens who did not interrupt their perpetual minuet, stepping forward and back, heel and toe, scratch and peck, scratch and peck, dipping to their partners. The kitchen was a typical bachelor affair: uncluttered and simply furnished. The lid of a black pot on the back of the wood stove jiggled noisily, emitting a fragrant aroma of stew which mingled with the sharp unmistakable smell of a crock of sourdough starter on the shelf above the stove. They sat at a table covered with faded oilcloth. Skip produced a bottle of tequila and two jelly glasses.

As they drank Skip told Roscoe how he had acquired the little ranch and of his discovery that the cattle which went with it had, for the most part, turned out to be wild and lived in the thickest brush down along the river.

"About then was when I went in the dog business," he said.

He explained that he had bought the first two dogs from a man who claimed that they were "genuine catahoola hog dogs" bred in Louisiana where they were used to catch the wild pigs which ran in the swamps and forests. By crossing those dogs with Australian Shepherds he had developed a strain which suited him and worked well catching the cattle in the thick brush. But even with the dogs there were some of the mustang cattle which he could not capture without help.

"When do we start?" Roscoe asked.

Skip got to his feet, grinning broadly, "Let's eat a little and sleep a while and start in the morning," he said.

Daylight found them bouncing along in Skip's old truck over a rough road which was little more than a path through the brush. On both sides ran an almost solid wall of gray-green mesquite, chaparral, and prickly pear. Occasionally a rabbit would dart out onto the road, change its mind, and duck back into the cover. The jungle of brush appeared impenetrable and as closely woven as a bird's nest of tough branches, twisted and thorned.

"This is going to be fun," Skip said.

"Yeah," Roscoe said, "like wrasseling buzz saws."

"Hell," Skip said, "if I was half as handy with a rope as you I wouldn't worry."

"If I was half as handy as you think I am I wouldn't worry, either."

"I guess you forget all the rope work I've seen you do," Skip said, wrenching at the wheel as the truck went into a hole in the road.

"Nobody but a pair of prize fools would go down into this kind of country and tie onto a half a ton of wild cow on purpose."

"Well," Skip said, "we've got the dogs. We'll let them do the dirty work. Besides, this kind of stuff is what keeps a man young."

"Or keeps him from living to get old," Roscoe said.

Skip laughed and swung the truck around another bend in the road. The old truck rattled on, and the two men were glad when they finally broke out into an abrupt clearing where there was a set of rough corrals. A windmill spun slowly above the twisted juniper fence.

"That's the outfit," Skip said. "The corrals are stouter than they look."

"They better be," Roscoe said.

They let down the tail gate on the rickety truck bed, and Skip's dogs tumbled out, chasing each other enthusiastically. Skip brought out two horses, and Roscoe led down Soldier and a little red mule with an elaborate Mexican brand on its shoulder.

"Come on, Enchilada," Roscoe said.

"Don't you be making fun of that mule," Skip called from the corral. "When you get in the brush you'll be glad you've got him."

They unloaded all their gear, and it was nearly dark by the time the pot of beans was bubbling over a hot little fire of brushwood. Roscoe and Skip squatted on their heels before the fire, passing a bottle of tequila back and forth. The half dozen dogs sprawled around them.

"Remember the time you roped that coyote when we were riding for the Hash Knife?" Skip said.

"Yeah. Like to scared that ringy old cook to death when I come busting into camp with it on the end of my string."

Skip rocked back with silent laughter. "You were yelling, 'Get a gun, get a knife, get a ax,' and all anybody would do was give you room."

"The things a kid won't do," Roscoe said.

They ate and then sat for a long time watching the fire burn itself into a heap of fine white ashes. Once in a while one or the other of them would push another stick into the embers and mention some common experience in their past.

"Remember old Scissor Bill Dedman?" Skip asked. "Remember when we went and hired on for the D's when he was wagon boss there?"

"Yeah," Roscoe said, looking down into the fire. "Old Bill comes out and looks us over and says, 'If either of you boys got any rabbit in you you better take it out and bury it before you draw a string on this outfit.' He was just about right, too."

"Lord-ee, yes," Skip said. "The meanest horses and the worst cook of any outfit I ever rode for."

Eventually they unrolled their beds and slept, dreaming of the days that would never come again, of the things that they would never do. Morning came soon.

For the next three days they rode together through the brushy bottom land along the dry riverbed, scouting for sign and studying the country. Each night they sat before a little fire and talked about the past.

"Well, Skipper," Roscoe said on the night of their third day of riding, "I think we got it figured. We've cut lots of sign and even though we haven't seen a hair on a cow it looks pretty good to me."

"Yep. The moon is coming on toward full and they'll be out feeding at night and holing up in the daytime."

Skip sketched a rough map of the area in the sandy earth.

"You want to try for that bunch we figure is in the lower draw in the morning?" he asked.

"Might just as well," Roscoe said.

Long before daylight, when the moon was still bright and high, they rode out from camp. Roscoe was on the red mule and Skip's dogs were trailing behind them. They rode as quietly as they could, seeking openings in the brush and working their way up into the wind. There was very little breeze stirring, but they were careful to keep it ahead of them. The dogs swung along with their heads low and seemed to understand the need for silence.

Roscoe shifted his weight, trying to get used to the mule's narrow barrel as the little animal moved in its peculiar choppy gait behind Skip's horse. The mule's long blunt ears flipped back and forth interestedly, and it seemed to know what was up.

The gray-green brush took on an eerie aspect in the moonlight and cast strange, distorted shadows. It was cool, and the full moon made it light enough to see. They rode on, and by the time the dipper had finished its circle of the north star and the morning star had begun to fade they had completed their detour, skirting the edge of one of the biggest clearings in the area. They stepped down and led their mounts to the fringe of the clearing.

Roscoe got down on his hands and knees as close to the ground as he could and tried to skylight out across the opening. Far out some vague, ghostly forms showed silhouetted against the milky night sky. A dog whined softly behind them, and Skip hissed at the sound, which stopped abruptly. They stood up and Skip pointed off to the right, swinging his arm in a wide circle back to the left. Roscoe nodded and mounted the mule.

As he rode away he let the mule have its head, giving him rein enough to pick his own way through the twisting trails. He loosened his ropes and built loops in both of them, and he could feel the mule's heart thudding under his leg. One rope Roscoe spooled and hung on his saddle horn with the loop doubled and tucked under the breast collar on the left side; the other rope he held ready with the coils of slack in his left hand with the reins, and the loop in his right. Both ropes were tied hard and fast at one end of the saddle horn.

Roscoe rode to the far end of the clearing and waited. The bitter scent of the brush around him mingled with the mule's pungent odor. The mule shifted nervously. Just a minute, Roscoe was thinking, just a minute now. He put his right hand with the loop of his first rope in it down against the little animal's bristly neck. He checked both ropes and slid his hand back to where the pigging strings were tucked under his belt. He had seen to his cinches. Everything was in order.

The mule began to nod his head up and down nervously, and Roscoe was trying to settle him when he heard the first thud of hooves sound hollowly out on the open ground. The mule shot out into the clearing almost before he was touched by the spurs.

A form, gray in the moonlight, loomed ahead, humped up and running. Roscoe stood in his stirrups. The mule was fine; his little legs pistoned up and down as he stretched into full stride and he brought Roscoe up to one of the running cattle. Roscoe lifted his arm and swung the loop, guessing at the target of bobbing horns.

Once, twice, and on the third swing he slapped the loop out and down, sending it straight ahead, flat and hard. He felt it go on. The mule kept pace with the brute and Roscoe flipped the slack of the rope over to the far side of the running form ahead so that the rope ran from the horns along the far side of its body. Roscoe reined the mule away to the left and at the same time put his weight on the left stirrup and turned his body to the right to look back down the rope. In the dim light he saw the slack pick up, coming to him from the far side of the cow just below the hocks.

The mule, moving away at an angle to the course of their quarry, stretched out his neck and plunged when he felt the rope grow taut. Roscoe saw the animal rise in the air as the rope lifted its hindquarters. The mule staggered, braced himself, and plunged again. The captive hit the ground after being flipped over; it hit hard with its head doubled back. Roscoe flung himself off the mule and stumbled toward what turned out to be a big roan cow.

As soon as he had tied the cow, Roscoe was back on the mule, spooling his rope as they ran. Brush crashed all around them as the wild cattle sought shelter, and the little mule galloped gamely along to dive into a thicket of twisted limbs. Roscoe lay low along the mule's neck, holding his loop doubled and in close. Something was just ahead but he could not tell what. He thought of all the stories he had heard about strange things which had been roped in the brush in the dark: bears, panthers, and such. A branch almost tore him from the saddle and another whipped across his face, leaving him blinded for a moment.

They broke into a pocket in the brush and Roscoe rose in time to see a yearling just ahead. Without opening the doubled loop he rose and pitched it overhand as if he were throwing a rock out in front of the animal and saw it unfold just in time. He jerked back on the slack and felt the loop take hold. The mule went to work, and just as the yearling was about to gain the far side of the pocket in the brush it was snapped up into the air and turned over to fall heavily on its back. Roscoe ran down the rope to make his tie. He remounted and turned back toward the sounds of the dogs. The mule was blowing hard.

In the big clearing it was coming to light, and he could make out that three of the dogs had a cow at bay. The cow, a lank Chihuahua type with wicked curling horns, stood with her head lowered, pivoting on her front feet, trying to hook the circling dogs. The dogs took turns dashing in to nip at her hocks from different sides.

Roscoe picked up his reins, and the mule went into its rolling run. The cow threw up her head at the sight of him and despite the dogs turned to bolt into the cover. Roscoe was on top of her before she got a good start and urged the mule right up beside her, even with her shoulder. He rolled his loop over the cow's withers so that it dropped neatly in front of her and caught her front feet. After jerking the loop tight, he took two quick turns around the saddle horn and rode away abruptly. The cow literally jumped into the air and spun over, landing very hard on her back. She gave a mighty grunt as the air was driven out of her lungs by the fall, and Roscoe was tying her feet before she realized what had happened.

Roscoe walked back to the mule, who was standing with his feet apart and his head down, dragging in deep breaths. The three dogs had disappeared and the sun was just coming up, throwing a lot of orange and violet light on the ragged clouds scattered all across the sky. Roscoe loosened the cinches on the mule and let him catch his breath.

They caught eight head of cattle that morning, and by dark had driven and dragged them into the corrals. The dogs sprawled in the dust at camp, happily tired, their tongues lolling and their little stumps of tails whisking back and forth. Roscoe drew several long ugly thorns out of the red mule's chest and shoulders and doctored the wounds while Skip fixed supper.

In the days that followed they repeated that morning's performance. Sometimes Roscoe rode Soldier, but while the horse was faster and stouter than the little mule he was nothing like as canny and quick in the brush, where most of the work had to be done. The dogs worked with consistent excellence, and it was not long before Roscoe knew them by name.

One old dog in particular, a header named Butch, attracted his attention. When the other dogs had forced one of the cattle out of cover by nipping at its heels, Butch would run up beside the animal and leap up to grab it by the muzzle. When he got a hold, Butch would flip himself into the air, throwing his full weight to one side. This usually snapped the cow's head to one side and threw it off stride, and Butch would be able to twist it to the ground. Butch would hold it there, and each time the cow tried to raise its head the old dog would growl through his clenched teeth and bear down on the tender muzzle. He would hold the animal until one of the men came to tie the cow down.

After a few treatments from Butch, even the wildest of the cattle could be driven in small bunches. In moving a small bunch, if the country were open enough, Butch would trot along in front while the other dogs got in behind and along the flanks with the two men. The heelers would dart in, nipping at the laggards while Butch held them down in front. If a critter showed any inclination toward running away, Butch would soon convince it of its error. Sometimes he could turn back an animal he had worked on simply by looking at it and clacking his teeth together.

One of the young dogs tried to stick with old Butch and seemed to want to work heads, too. Once the young dog, Buster, had thrown a yearling imitating Butch's technique, and the old dog had simply sat by and watched, honoring his catch so to speak, but for the most part Butch showed little patience with the younger dog and ran him off when he got in the way.

Buster was much more friendly toward the men than Butch, who maintained a studied independence, and often in the evening the young dog would come and lay his head in Roscoe's lap to be petted and to have the burrs taken out of the long hair around his ears. Butch's mane and ears became matted and knotty with stickers, but he would slink off when he saw Skip take out his long-bladed knife and begin cleaning up one of the other dogs.

"That Butch, now," Skip said, "he's all business. Always has been. He just kind of puts up with me, lets me feed him and acts like he doesn't much care if I do or not. All he wants to do in this life is eat up on cattle."

"It looks like," Roscoe said, "maybe the Australian Shepherd you bred into the others civilized them a little."

"Yeah," Skip said. "They're a good cross."

The dogs took some punishment from the wild cattle, kicks and hornings, but they were never daunted. "Get a holt!" Skip would shout. "You Dixie. Grab beef! Get a holt!" The dogs would swarm all over the cattle, grabbing at the loose hide, the ears, tail, anywhere they could.

Once they jumped a small bunch of cattle on their way back to camp in full daylight after an unsuccessful morning. The multicolored cattle dove into a thicket where the men and horses could not follow and lay down deep in the brush facing their back trail. It was frustrating because Roscoe and Skip circled the thicket and knew that they were still in there and they could see no way to get at them; but they had dealt with squatters of that sort before.

"Roscoe," Skip called, "keep Butch and that Buster dog with you. I'll send the heelers in."

Roscoe called the two dogs out into the clearing where they lay down behind the mule, whining softly.

Skip and the other four dogs disappeared around the thicket and Roscoe could hear him urging them on. It was scorching hot in the open, but Roscoe knew that it was even hotter in the chaparral and mesquite where the air did not circulate at all. Roscoe built his loops and checked his cinches and listened to Skip talking to the dogs. Abruptly the tone of Skip's voice changed.

"Take to 'em," Skip yelled. "Take holt! Eat 'm up!"

The dogs began whining. Roscoe hissed at them and they were still.

Suddenly the wall of thorns parted and a big black and white bull charged out with three dogs hanging to him. One dog, the little bitch Dixie, had a mouthful of the wrinkled hide on the bull's shoulder, another dog hung from the opposite flank, and the third had a firm grip on one of the bull's hocks. As soon as the bull got well clear of the thicket, the dogs dropped off and circled the big humped animal, who lowered his wickedly curved horns and made a rush at Dixie. The little blue and gray dog dodged nimbly aside as her two teammates rushed at the bull's hindquarters, snapping and barking.

The spotted bull wheeled to face them, and as he did Dixie darted in low on the ground and, twisting her head, closed her jaws very deliberately on his hind leg. The startled bull kicked, but Dixie had flattened herself to the ground well out of range. The dogs kept the bull bayed and pivoting in a small circle. If the big animal stood quietly the three dogs would flop to their bellies in the ring around him, but the instant he showed signs of moving they would rise to a low coyote-like crouch, waiting to see which direction he planned to take and then begin harassing him until he stood his ground.

Roscoe knew that he would not be able to rope and throw the big animal alone because the mule was tired, and so was he, so he sat with his rope ready, waiting for Skip. Behind him the brush crashed again, and a cow rushed out with the fourth dog hanging from her neck like a dewlap. Realizing that the single dog would not be able to hold the cow, Roscoe swung out of the saddle quickly and grabbed young Buster by the loose hide at the back of his neck.

"Butch," Roscoe said, and the old dog looked up eagerly. "Go get him!"

Roscoe swept his free hand in the direction of the watchful bull, and Butch hurled himself off toward the black and white outlaw. Buster whined and trembled in Roscoe's grasp. Turning the young dog toward the cow who was circling wildly, trying to hook the dog that had driven her from cover, Roscoe released him with a "Sic 'em, Buster."

The black and blue spotted shepherd raced frantically toward the cow, and Roscoe stepped up onto the waiting mule, gathering his rope and reins. Before Roscoe reached the cow, Buster had it on the ground and Roscoe made short work of tying it. When he straightened up he saw that the bull was down as well. Butch lay at the bull's head with his jaws closed firmly over the tender muzzle, while the other dogs lay in a circle around them. Skip came around the far side of the thicket and reached the bull ahead of Roscoe.

"Let's tie him," Skip said. "There's three more in there."

By dark they had all five of the bunch in the corrals. Buster had watched his personal cow all the way into the pens, and he seemed almost disappointed that she had not made a bid for freedom. That evening the young dog came to Roscoe several times to be reminded of how well he had done on the cow. Old Butch lay outside the circle of firelight growling quietly in his sleep.

"We'll go to town tomorrow," Skip said, "and send the trucks out for this collection."

Roscoe nodded.

"I'm worn to a frazzle," he said. "Time was when I could keep this up forever. Now just this little bit and I hurt all over. That mule gets taller everytime I go to get back on him."

"I've slowed down considerable myself," Skip said. "The last day or so I even got to hoping we wouldn't find any more."

Roscoe nodded.

"You reckon there's many left in the brush, Skip?"

"Naw. Can't be many left and they're so spooked by now we probably couldn't get within a mile of them."

"Leave them for seed," Roscoe said quietly.

"What?"

"Leave a few for seed stock," Roscoe said. "Catch them all and what would we do for fun the next time?"

"That's right," Skip said. "Won't be long before knowing how to catch wild cattle won't mean much 'cause there won't be any."

Roscoe stared blankly at the fire.

"I remember," he said, "when I was just a button of a kid, my dad telling me about the old days when they made up a herd to drive north. It must have been about like this. He said it was more like rounding up a bunch of deer."

After a long silence Roscoe went on:

"A man ought to have sons, Skip. A man ought to have sons so he can tell them the things he's learned. Pretty quick now there's not going to be anybody around to tell the beginners what they need to know. Like how they should always loosen a horse's cinch before they go to swim him, and they should bed a herd on the far side of water, and coal oil will loosen burrs, and bluestone will keep down proud flesh and cure hoof rot, and a light rope is best for heeling. You know. All like that that nobody much knows anymore."

"Likely nobody will need to know before long," Skip said. "We're getting old, Roscoe. No two ways about it. They got squeeze chutes now, dodge gates, calf tables, hot shots, jeeps. Don't much need our kind."

"Maybeso," Roscoe grumbled, "but people have been telling me that all my life and I've managed to get along. I remember people saying the same about my dad. If I'd of raised a son I'd of made sure he knew the things people like us know. Not just how to part cows and calves, but what it takes to be a man, what his word was worth, and things that really matter."

Chapter 16

<And then one day I woke up an old man. Oh, I guess it had been coming on, but I never paid much attention. When I started to think about it it bothered me at first. I thought about all the things I'd never do again, the things I'd never see. It took me awhile to get used to the idea.>

HE WAS WORKING for the VB again. Jack Hastings, Buck's son, was bossing the crew, and they were busy getting ready for winter. One of the annual chores involved bringing the range bulls down from the mountains to headquarters. Roscoe twisted in his saddle to look back at the herd of Hereford bulls moving steadily, bugling and moaning, through the afternoon heat. There was no wind and the dust settled upon them. Dust exploded around each broad-splayed hoof and drifted back, sometimes hanging lightly in wisps along the flanks of the big animals, sometimes rising in a breeze that was never felt. Behind them rose the peaks of their summer range mountains, and ahead, below the gold, autumn color of the aspen groves, was the home ranch where they would winter.

Jack Hastings slack-reined his big-boned sorrel out around the herd and rode up beside Roscoe.

"A good gather, Roscoe," he said in his deep, gentle voice.

"We're shy one?" Roscoe asked, and Jack nodded.

"Well," Roscoe said, "I'll go back up and set all the water traps and bring him down with eight or ten cows."

"Yeah," Jack said. "I noticed a while back, when we were parting out the dry cows, that there were some of

170

the older cows as needed hooves trimmed and horns tipped. Might be you could use them for bringing down the bull. We'd doctor them in the squeeze."

Roscoe nodded, but his automatic contempt for squeeze chutes rose like a bad taste in his mouth.

"Yeah," he said. "The ride back up to camp will give me a chance to try that gray colt in the open."

"You forget about that colt," Jack said and reined away.

The bulls plodded on, moaning and grunting. The men did not try to hurry them, for they knew that bulls will not be hurried. Occasionally one of the bulls would pause and twist awkwardly to lick at the clusters of flies on its broad back, or bellow toward the cool hills, where, long before dawn, the men had ridden out from Roscoe's little line camp and gathered them from their various bed-grounds to start them down the trail. Now they were almost to the pasture headquarters where the bulls would spend the winter and be fed by the men who stayed at the ranch.

All but me, Roscoe thought. Thank God for winter camp where a man can be alone. Another month in the mountains and then out to the desert with the cows for the winter.

Roscoe reined his sleepy horse down the arroyo which the trail had become and led the herd, twisting out through the last of the foothills. The flats of red earth were dotted with greasewood and sage. A windmill in the distance marked the entrance to the pasture, and the older bulls made toward it, moving a little faster, bellowing now toward the smell of water. Jack loped ahead to let down the gate, his sorrel horse floating along in that almost somnolent gait characteristic of range horses. Jack sat easily in the saddle, and the horse, carrying its head level with the saddle horn, seemed to be falling forward, barely catching itself with each stride.

Roscoe watched him go toward the windmill, tiny in the distance and spinning lazily atop its spidery frame, marking the entrance to the pasture. Thank the Lord, he thought, this country is good for nothing, good for nothing but cows. If they could figure out anything else to use it for it'd be the end of the cow business. Leastwise, the end of it the way I know it, and I'm too old to learn my way around feed lots and irrigated pastures.

He was saddened by the thought that the skills he had spent a lifetime perfecting were dropping in value, were no longer in much demand, just as he had been dismayed by the fact that he seemed to approach each day with an accumulating fatigue.

"But I'll show them a thing or two with that colt," he said aloud and looked around quickly to see if he had been overheard.

Ever since Soldier's death in a rodeo barn fire Roscoe had been searching for a young horse to train as a replacement. Until now he had not found one that suited him.

I'll show these dirt farmers that what the years may take out of your muscles gets moved up to your head, where it counts. I'll be taking that gray back up this trail in a day or two or know the reason why. Jack's a good boy. He ain't Buck's son for nothing. He'll come around.

Once in the field the bulls watered and spread out to graze as the men rode west toward the ranch buildings. It was nearly dark when they reached the corrals, and the cook grudgingly built up his fire to feed them. Roscoe listened to the rest of the crew talking at supper. Young Pete, the pimply-faced kid, showed a mouthful of half-chewed food as he poked loud fun at one of the older men, then he closed his mouth and his prominent Adam's apple bobbed as he swallowed. Snotty kid, Roscoe thought, doesn't know enough to know he doesn't know a goddamn thing.

In the bunkhouse Jack pointed out a spare bedroll to Roscoe, who had left his at the line camp, knowing that he would be back. It was part of the gear that a cowboy had left behind a few weeks earlier when he had failed to return from a trip to town. Rumor had it that he had joined a movie crew at work south of town. He was the hand who had started the gray colt Roscoe coveted, and since he was obviously gone for good Roscoe saw no reason why he could not take over the colt's education.

He sat on the edge of the bunk and thought with

pleasure of just how he would go about training the handsome young horse. Before going to bed he went outside to urinate. It was a clear night, and the plain was all silver and blue in the moonlight. The bulls bellowed out in the darkness. Coming back around the bunkhouse, he passed an open window and heard young Pete's voice saying:

"Thank God he ain't going to winter here. This shack smells like a bear's armpit anyhow without that old goat adding to it. And he's so goddamn set in his ways."

"Leave off," Jack said. "He may smell kind of rank and he may not be easy for the likes of you to get on with, but he forgets more about cows every day before breakfast than you'll ever know. Deal. One more round and I'm turning in."

Roscoe turned away from the window and walked slowly down to the corrals. Only one horse, kept in for wrangling the others in the morning, stood by the hayracks, hipshot and slack-eared. Roscoe leaned against the fence and looked across the flats to the mountains with their perpetually snow-capped peaks shining in the moonlight.

Times have changed, he thought, but then they've got a right to. Come spring I'll be what, sixty-five or -six? Time was when a man rode for this outfit he was in good company. Good men. The best. Now? Dirt farmers and green kids. It takes a lot of the pride out of the work. If it wasn't for Jack Hastings, Roscoe Banks would be hard to find around this spread.

He knew what was eating Pete. The kid wanted that gray colt. He wanted him but he couldn't ask for him because he had been complaining about the fact that he had so many green horses in his string. Roscoe had jobbed him one day when Pete let some cattle get away. He said he didn't think Pete could herd chickens. Pete had turned to Jack and said he wished, he just wished, that there was somebody else on the ranch able to do their work on young horses the way he always had to. Well, Roscoe said to himself, we'll just see about that.

He turned and made his way slowly up the slope to

the bunkhouse. Somewhere to the south a coyote yapped three short barks and then was still.

On the way into town the next day Roscoe sat in the cab of the pickup with Jack while Elmer, Duke, and Pete rode in the back.

"I'll be needing some grub for camp," Roscoe said, and Jack nodded.

"We'll get that first thing," Jack answered. "I'll break off part of that forequarter that's in the meat safe for you, too."

Jack drove down through the red rock canyon, and neither man spoke for some time. Roscoe was making out a list of supplies in his head.

"What have you got up there for horseflesh, Roscoe?" Jack asked abruptly.

"I got the old bay that I rode down: Freckles," he said. "He's getting awful stiff in front. Hates to turn downhill."

He paused and saw Jack nod.

"Then there's that Doctor Runyan pinto," he went on. "He's stout enough but a awful dummy."

Jack was grinning at the memory of the clowning pinto.

"I'm of a mind to take that gray colt Jim started up and start him on cattle. Work him out some this winter and make a horse of him by spring," Roscoe said.

"Hell, Roscoe," Jack protested. "He's nothing more than green broke. Take a horse you can count on. You'll be by yourself."

Roscoe shook his head. "I fancy that colt," he said.

"He's awkward," Jack said. "Hasn't got his feet under him. No rein. Nothing. Sure, he's well made and gentle, but you don't want to be fooling around with him up in the hills by yourself."

"He'll learn," Roscoe said.

"Look, Roscoe," Jack said. "You've done your bronc stomping and we all know it. You don't have to prove a damn thing to me. Maybe you forget, but I've seen you and my dad work horses every day of the week that these jokers couldn't even bridle."

"Yes," Roscoe said slowly, "I know. But when the day

comes that I figure I'm past bringing on any more young horses I'm going to spool my bed and head for town so the bookkeeper can figure my time, Jack. There's lots of things changed about the cow business, but you still need men and horses to run this outfit and I'm a man that likes to sharpen his own tools."

Jack shook his head, but Roscoe knew that the colt was his.

The next day Jack helped Roscoe pack his supplies. They loaded the kyaks and hung them on Doctor Runyan, a platter-footed pinto. Roscoe caught and saddled Freckles, and without a word went back into the corral and skillfully roped a sturdy gray colt out of the remuda. He mounted and, taking the lead rope from Jack, started away. He shoved his feet deeper into the stirrups and straightened in the saddle as he passed the other men. They paused in their work, and Roscoe felt them watching him.

"Hold back on his feed, Pop," Pete called after him, "and he won't generate no notions."

Roscoe's face burned with anger but he made no reply.

It was almost dark when he reached the little line camp. He turned the horses into the pole corral, fed them, and stacked his supplies neatly in the cabin. After eating some stale biscuits with jam, he went to bed without building a fire.

Roscoe woke slowly, lifting himself from sleep with an effort. The cabin was dark and cold. It was not time to get up, but his dream had reached an impasse and the effort of trying to get over it woke him. He tasted his mouth and stretched, testing his bad hip to see how much it was going to plague him through the coming day. A man gets old, he told himself, a man gets old and all the hurts add up: the years of getting bucked off and kicked, the sleeping on the ground and riding in the snow, the little hurts you pay no heed when you are young and supple. They all come back and stiffen you through the long winters.

He burrowed down into his blankets, savoring their

warmth. After all, there was no need to get up. He was alone and could relax.

"Nothing to get up for except my bladder," he muttered, "and it's just going to have to wait."

The wind began and grew gradually stronger, moaning in the flue, warning Roscoe that the sun would soon ease itself up between the 'Frisco Peaks. He stretched again, and this time his hip popped comfortably. Today he would set the trap gates to the water lots and catch the renegade bull. He's probably in the neighborhood of the Bill Williams tank, he thought. Blast the contrary critter anyway, hiding out when we gathered the others. Serve him right to let him stay out all winter while the rest are being fed.

Now the wind soughed loudly through the pines around the cabin, causing them to creak like the timbers of a ship, and Roscoe watched the first true light slant through the window and touch the scrollwork on the side of his squat wood stove. He swung his union-suited legs out of the blankets and pulled on a pair of dirt-stiffened Levis. Once dressed, he hurried outside. The sun was balanced on the mountain peak, big and red and warm looking, but Roscoe shivered in the cold morning air. A horse nickered in the corral.

"Wait, damn you," Roscoe said. "I got to make a fire."

He went back into the cabin and fumbled through the woodbox to find a pitchy knot for a starter. As he pushed the wood into the belly of the little stove he chuckled and said aloud, "Liked to scared that kid Pete to death, when he first came and I had him up here. The fuss I raised about the firewood when he cut it too long for the stove. Him sitting way back so he wouldn't have to act like he noticed and me a-hammering on every piece to show it wouldn't go in and then throwing them one at a time out the door."

He laughed again and let the stove lid crash back into place. It was going to be pleasant to have a camp all to himself again, he thought. By yourself there's no need for talk, no need to look like you're doing something all the time. A man can sit in the doorway on a warm evening and watch the shadows move down the hills, and whether there's a hot meal or not won't matter. The work will get done, but it won't have to be done just so.

One by one he mixed mush, prunes, and coffee, and when the fire was roaring in the chimney he took his duck-covered mackinaw from its hook on the door and went out again. In the corral the three horses watched him limp toward them. The old bay whinnied in anticipation and shook his bony head violently up and down while the pinto and the gray nickered softly.

"Act like you haven't eaten in a month," Roscoe grumbled and began tossing hay into the feed rack.

When he finished he leaned against the corral fence and studied the colt. The gray raised its head with wisps of hay sticking from its mouth and stared back.

"Maybe I've got no business fooling with you, young feller," Roscoe said aloud. "But I'd just like to ride you into headquarters next spring and show them what a real cow horse looks like."

He limped back to the cabin and ate. Breakfast is a sorry meal, he thought as he washed the few dishes. When he got back to the corral the horses were finished with the hay and were waiting to see which of them was going to be worked. The pinto wormed his way around behind the colt and pretended to be very interested in something on the far side of the corral. The old bay and the colt followed Roscoe with their eyes as he went into the shed and brought out his saddle, bridle, and catch rope. They watched him enter the corral, drop his saddle, and shake out a loop in the rope. The pinto dropped his head and intently examined the base of the corral post, blowing up little puffs of dust with his breath. Roscoe stood for a moment with the rope ready in his hands. Freckles twitched his ears forward and a muscle in the colt's neck began to dance.

Look at him, Roscoe was thinking, look at the slope of his shoulders and the way his head is set on his neck. He's too good for the likes of that Pete. Besides, all that gunsel can do is put a fast rein on a horse, working him dry, and get him all razzed up and what have you got then?

Roscoe raised his arm and shot the loop out without any warning. It settled over the gray colt's head and snapped up tight, behind the jaw where it belonged. The young horse snorted and stood with his legs braced for a moment, trembling, before he stepped toward Roscoe. The old bay trotted away shaking his head, and the pinto made a great show of the sudden discovery that Roscoe was in the corral.

The colt stood quietly while Roscoe saddled him. He had seen the colt ridden and knew that it was gentle, but he moved slowly, letting it get used to the idea of being handled all over again. He stepped up into the saddle and winced as he lifted his bad leg over the cantle. The gray answered the reins awkwardly and turned toward the end of the long meadow.

"Come on, little hoss," Roscoe said. "Let's go find a bull."

Roscoe guided the young horse out into the meadow and toward a trail through the woods. He let the colt pick its own way through the big timber as they worked across the mountain. In the pines there was no undergrowth, but wherever the big trees let even a small spot of sunlight through to the ground a dozen seeds had germinated and were sending up small trees toward the patch of open sky.

The colt clumsily caught a hoof in a rotten windfall, and Roscoe cursed as he braced himself too late to avoid being jolted. He pulled the snorting horse up and continued carefully until they were out of the timber, through a jungle of jack pine, and on a solid trail. The ground grew rockier, and when Roscoe turned the colt up a steep bare slope the young horse stopped and turned as though he wanted to go back. While Roscoe was patiently trying to force him up the grade a bull bugled in a distant canyon.

"That's him, hoss," he said excitedly. "Get at it!"

The colt floundered up through the rocks, scaring Roscoe at the ungainly way he handled himself and how close he came to falling. But the bull roared again, and Roscoe hurried the colt on. A hawk soared past and

Roscoe watched it drop screaming over the crest of the hill.

Once over the hill Roscoe let the colt down through the rimrock to a trail which led to the Bill Williams tank. The tank was a fenced water lot containing a shallow pond which had been scooped out in the bottom of a natural basin. Dirt had been pushed up into a horseshoe-shaped dam which caught the runoff from thawing mountain snow and infrequent summer thunderstorms. Now, in the fall of the year, the water was low and brackish, but it was water; the only water for miles. The cattle had long since grazed the hills around the tank bare and now they came only to drink and rest and drink again before they drifted back up into the mountains where they could still find feed. To the south Roscoe could see several small groups of cows grazing their way along trails toward the water lot.

The gate leading into the tank consisted of three short lengths of pipe hung horizontally inside the heavy gate-posts. They were tied back now, and the cattle could come and go at will, but when Roscoe let them swing shut and attached the spring they would be able only to push their way in and not out. The trap set, he turned the colt up the draw to cover where he could wait for his quarry because the bull was on his way in to drink.

First a group of five cows plodded into the canyon and shoved their way through the gate. They drank and stood placidly in the water swishing at flies with their tails. Then seven more cows joined them, and as Roscoe watched from his hiding place a full-grown whiteface bull walked deliberately up the brush-lined trail toward the water lot. His voice rumbled deep in his chest and his heavy horns swayed to the rhythm of his gait. "Uhhhmm," he muttered. "Uhhh." Over and over.

Once in the clearing, he paused and tipped up his nose to bellow a long bugling challenge, which started out hoarse and rumbling, like summer thunder in the mountains, and ended in a high-pitched blast. He repeated it three times, stood for a moment waiting to hear an answer, and when all that came was what the canyon walls threw back at him with mocking overtones, he resumed his ponderous pace "Uhhh. Uhhh. Uhhhmm." The colt shook its head impatiently, and Roscoe dropped a hand to its neck to steady it. Again the bull roared his challenge, full of sullen rage and defiance. It went unanswered and he proceeded truculently up the slope.

Before he reached the gate he paused at an old wallow and kneeled to rub his shoulders against the bank. The red soil clung to his brisket and streaked the white along his heavy neck. He rose from his knees and hooked his right horn into the earth, withdrew it and hooked again, chopping hard and grunting with the impact. With a long pawing stroke, his splayed hoof flipped dirt high in the air so that it came down on his back and neck, disturbing clusters of flies and darkening the curly hair on his broad forehead. He kneeled again and rubbed his shoulders, rumbling and mumbling to himself.

Roscoe watched him, smiling and thinking: You're sure proud, aren't you, bully, ready to take on the world? It's a mighty dirty trick you're going to get played on you, but this old life is full of dirty tricks.

After a few more thrusts of his horns and with much bellowing and muttering, the bull proceeded to the water lot and pushed his way in. The cows watched him approach, plodding majestically and growling under his breath. They watched him drink, sucking up long swallows. He drank until his flanks filled out and the water began to swell the dry grass in his stomach, then he marched up the bank and lay down.

Wait awhile, Roscoe thought, wait and let him drink again. With a good bellyful he won't want to go on the prod or prance around when I go to move him.

The bull closed his eyes and dozed, ruminating, while Roscoe watched. The sun moved steadily across the canyon, shifting the shadows of the fence posts. A hawk wheeled effortlessly in lazy circles overhead, and Roscoe studied it as it hung for a moment etched against the rich blue sky and then plunged at some target below. Then the hawk spiraled upward, screaming its piercing cry, wheeled again and tipped a wing down to knife into the updraft from the canyon.

Finally the bull pushed himself to his feet with a grunt and went to the water for another drink. Roscoe rode out of the brush and into the trap. The cattle moved away from him as he sat for a moment looking at the bull.

There's time enough, he was thinking, with just this little bunch, to make it down to the ranch, if I take a couple of shortcuts. I should have help, but I can do it. Show those bastards down below what a good man can get done even with a green colt. Shut them up for a while. It would tickle Jack too.

He tied the bars of the gate back and circled the cattle in the lot. The cows that were not already on their feet humped themselves up hind end first. They filed out of the gate, the bull in the lead, and turned up toward a memory of feed in the high country. With only a few deft maneuvers and feints, Roscoe swung them back and started them down the long trail to the home ranch.

With cattle in front of him, the colt began to show interest in his work; he flattened his ears against his neck and nipped at the stragglers. Roscoe grinned and let him have plenty of rein. At first the cattle did not move as a herd, but individually, and it was hard to keep them bunched. When they got into the rocks they sulled and on open ground they tried to scatter, but gradually they settled down and accepted control. The bull's gait was slower than that of the cows and soon he had to labor to keep up.

Roscoe had decided to try the pass on Cedar Mountain. It was narrow and steep, but it would cut miles off the route they had taken with the big herd. The colt was working well but awkwardly. They pushed ahead. When they reached the rocky wash which was the bottom of the trail to the pass, Roscoe rode around the cattle and turned them up the draw. It was slow going because of the slides and loose rocks, but the herd went along and the colt struggled over the rough ground.

Nearing the summit the trail turned into a narrow ledge, forcing the cattle into single file. Rock slides slashed the face of the canyon walls. Several times the colt floundered, and Roscoe juggled his weight in the saddle. I ought to get down and lead him, he thought. A young horse has trouble enough handling himself in bad places like this without a man's weight unbalancing him. But if I climb through here afoot I'll be stiff for a week. He stayed in the saddle and urged the colt on.

Then one of the colt's front feet became wedged between two boulders and he shrugged. As he pitched forward Roscoe knew that the gray had gotten its front legs crossed and though he was scrambling frantically he could not save himself from falling. Roscoe tried to push himself out of the saddle as the side of the hill slipped away, but as if in slow motion and with each detail clear in his mind, he saw that he was not going to get free before the weight of the horse caught up with him. He tried to hurry. He heard the rattle of falling rocks, glimpsed a view of blue sky, and then was hit from both sides at once.

Each time he floated to the surface of consciousness some heavy weight would push him down again until he forgot why he had been trying to get up and let the weight, force, whatever it was, shove him deeper into the darkness full of swimming red blots. I'll just rest a little longer, he told himself, there's no big hurry. But there seemed a reason why he should get up, so he pushed against the weight holding him until the red parallelograms whirled faster and faster and the taste of blood and dirt filled his mouth. Still, he was surprisingly numb. There should be pain, he thought, but I can't even tell where I'm hurt. A kaleidoscope of red and green wedges against a background of black started changing patterns, and as the darkness began to smother the design he realized that he was alone, with no one to help him. He struggled against the weight in one brief, desperate effort. In the distance it seemed he could hear the bawling of thirsty cattle.

"Ruby?" he muttered. "So much blood."

Gradually he returned to consciousness and, one limb

at a time, became aware of his position; he was on his back, pinned under the colt who lay with its feet pointing up the rocky slope. Instinctively Roscoe was clutching the headstall to keep the horse's head twisted back toward the saddle horn, preventing him from rising. I can't let him up, he thought, my foot that's under him may likely be hung up some way and he'd drag or stomp me. For a long time he lay there taking stock, grimly clinging to the bridle.

The colt was breathing and struggled now and then. Each time he wallowed on Roscoe's leg he ground it against the rocks. Still, there was only a remote kind of pain; that part of his body felt disconnected from the rest of him. This sort of thing has happened before, he was thinking, and there are all kinds of ways of getting out of it. If I could get at my pocket knife I could cut the latigo on the top side, and when I let him up me and the saddle would stay here. That would work just fine, but the knife is in the pocket that's under him. If I can reach the cinch ring maybe I can untie the latigo.

He moved slowly, twisting the upper part of his body and gritting his teeth against the pain that came surging up. At last he was able to change hands on the headstall. Then, being careful to hold the colt's head well back, he groped for the strap that held the cinch. He stretched to the utmost but was unable to reach the rigging. Exhausted, he lay back and tried to think of something else. His mouth was dry and his temples throbbed. The colt's flanks pumped desperately. Maybe he'll die, Roscoe thought, a horse can't live long on its back. Maybe I can take a rock in my free hand and club him. He reached behind himself and searched the ground for a loose rock but could not find one large enough. Anyway, he thought, how would I get out from under him if I did knock him out?

"Well," he said to himself, "fifty years of saddle work should give a man savvy enough to get out of this sort of jackpot, if you don't have sense enough to stay out of it in the first place."

It was nearly dark when the colt began to struggle fran-

tically. He must be fixing to pass out, Roscoe thought;
I've got to do something. He weighed the possibilities and
decided that he would have to gamble on the chance that
his imprisoned leg might not be snarled in the stirrup or
cinch. It was the only way out. Let him up, he decided,
and hang on to the reins. If your foot or spur are hung,
you're a dead man, but if they're not you may make it.
He looked around, trying to determine the probable
direction the colt's feet would take and then, tightly grip-
ping the end of one rein, he let the colt have its head.

For an instant the panting gray lay still and then he
surged and struggled, mashing Roscoe's leg into the rocks
until he got his front feet under him and thrust his fore-
quarters off the ground. Roscoe watched the saddle rise
as he pushed it away with his free foot.

The colt came up clear and lunged. Roscoe clung grimly
to the rein with both hands as the colt dragged him a
short way down the hill before he was able to make the
young horse turn and face him. He lay still and heard the
rocks bounce down to the bottom of the canyon and then
he raised his head. The colt stood at the end of the taut
rein with its head down and nostrils flaring with spas-
modic breaths.

It was some time before Roscoe could summon the
strength to drag himself toward the trembling animal,
and when he did the colt snorted and drew back. Again
and again Roscoe slowly and painfully approached, and
always the colt backed away. It was completely dark by
the time he reached the bridle, and it took the last
reserve of his strength to pull himself up the stirrup. He
leaned against the saddle, gasping with pain, the taste of
bile in his mouth, and then, with an effort of which he
no longer thought himself capable, he dragged his broken
body into the saddle.

His injured leg dangled uselessly down the stirrup
leather as the colt picked its way through the pass and
down into the open country on the other side. "Thank
the Lord for a moon," Roscoe muttered as they emerged
onto a greasewood mesa. Just then he saw the cattle he

had been driving bedded down on the flat. The colt saw them at the same time and turned toward them.

"What do you think, son?" Roscoe said. "You haven't got a bellyful yet?"

The cattle began humping themselves to their feet as, whistling and cursing, Roscoe roused them and started them down the trail out of the foothills, the bull in the lead. They moved along sullenly at first, and then one old cow, sensing that she might be going back to her weaned calf, swung into a trail gait and Roscoe urged the spent colt after them.

"Let's take them in, little hoss," he said quietly.

Breakfast was on the long table in the cook shack at headquarters and the crew were just sitting down when Elmer looked out toward the corral and started.

"What's that at the gate?" he said.

Jack looked and was out the door before anyone else. He ran to the corral and stopped to approach the tired colt cautiously, talking in low soothing tones. Roscoe was slumped forward on the horn of his saddle. Jack lifted the old man gently down and carried him toward the pickup truck. The other men came forward hesitantly, solemn in the presence of what looked like death.

"Pete," Jack said sharply, "start the truck. Elmer, get two bedrolls and put them in the back. Duke, the cook's got a bottle hid somewhere; get it."

Once directed, the men moved quickly, and while Jack cradled the unconscious Roscoe lightly in his arms they did as they were told. The bulky tarp-covered bedrolls were spread out in the back of the pickup, filling the bed, and Jack gently eased Roscoe down onto them and pillowed his head. The cook himself came out with his bottle and handed it up to Jack, but after one brief glance at Roscoe's queerly twisted leg, now so swollen that it stretched the seams of his pants, the cook turned quickly away.

"All right, Pete," Jack said. "Point this thing toward town. Easy on the bumps, but get us there quick."

The young man nodded and stepped into the truck.

As they swung out of the gate Jack carefully spilled a little of the whiskey into Roscoe's mouth. The old man coughed, swallowed, and then opened his eyes. He said nothing for a moment and then motioned for another drink. Again he coughed.

"That bull's in the lower field with the rest," he said with great effort. "I brought him in. There's a dozen cows with him."

Jack nodded and signaled him to lie back and relax, and Roscoe closed his eyes. Later, when they were nearing town, he opened his eyes again and put his hand on Jack's arm. Jack lifted the bottle, but Roscoe motioned it away.

"You take the gray colt," Roscoe said. "He's got all the makings of a real stock horse."

Chapter 17

WHEN HE WAS finally discharged from the hospital in Flagstaff, Roscoe withdrew to Coconino and took up residence in Mrs. Brady's boardinghouse. Waiting for his "strength to come back" was his explanation, but everyone knew that he had ridden out after his last cow.

The old man became a familiar figure limping along the sidewalk, with a cane at first and then shakily without it, sitting with two or three other old-timers on the green benches in front of the post office, or lounging in a wooden chair just inside the big doors of Bud Stacy's garage.

He and his fellow boarders at Mrs. Brady's spun yarns during the long evenings when they rocked endlessly together on the porch in the summer and in the front parlor during the cold weather. They gave every appearance of listening to one another, they nodded and exclaimed in the right places and remained silent when they should. When one would finish an anecdote the others would support whatever point the narrator had been trying to make with illustrations from their own experience. For a time they would sit in silence while each of them searched his mind for the memory of a tale which they had heard so long ago that it had become something that happened to them and they could tell it in the first person. They heard one another out politely without listening. They encouraged one another to talk on so that when it came their turn they would have an audience. No one else would hear them, so they heard one another.

Two of his cronies were retired railroad men, one a mill hand, and one a grocer from the East who had turned his store over to his son and come to Arizona "for his health." Their stories were rambling and often seemed pointless, but somehow the teller always managed to wind up with a moral which would draw nods of approval.

Of the five, Roscoe was the only one who did not admit that his active life was over. He referred often to the time when he would "get back to work." And, indeed, he was the most active of them all. He did odd jobs around town and assumed the position of honorary constable. The obvious lack of any need for a law-enforcement agency in quiet little Coconino did not embarrass him. He looked in at the two bars almost daily to assure himself that no trouble was brewing and jotted down the license numbers of any out-of-state cars he saw. He studied the wanted bulletins in the post office and covertly searched the faces of tourists for any resemblance.

The post office was his favorite hangout. Jenny and Martha Moore, the old-maid sisters who owned the little building and served as the postal staff, doted on Roscoe. When a window stuck or a hinge squeaked they turned very feminine and helpless. Roscoe could be counted on to come to their rescue. When a rare special delivery or registered item came in the mail, Roscoe was always ready to search out its addressee and secure signatures on the proper forms. This last assignment he carried out with all the dignity and seriousness of a diplomat delivering an official note.

"The girls," as Roscoe referred to Jenny and Martha, said they did not know what they would do without him. Jenny, the older of the "girls" by a matter of five or six years, never ceased to surprise most people by her kittenish attitude toward Roscoe because in all other matters she appeared to be eminently self-sufficient. Martha, who had been dominated and led by her sister all through life, had been told that she was a silly for so long that she had come to believe it and behave so; yet Jenny confessed once that it was Martha who kept the books and made up the reports which were required of them. But in public Jenny ridiculed Martha's blushes and called her an "empty-headed ninny."

Whatever their true relationship, the two of them made much over Roscoe and each behaved toward him in a way that made the old fellow proud and happy.

So it was that Roscoe lived out his last days, helping his "girls," answering the phone in Bud Stacy's combination garage-smithy-machine shop, explaining himself to his friends, and guarding the well-established peace of Coconino as a self-appointed but recognized authority. He became accepted by all and loved by many of the town's 284 citizens; and when he was killed almost the entire population followed his coffin up the slope north of town to see him safely laid to rest among the cedars.

It started this way: two young men who had been working on a construction job for the state highway department in the southern part of the state were fired when they were caught stealing gasoline from the storage tanks on the job. Charges were not brought against them because the matter was thought to be too insignificant. They headed north in their battered gray coupe, pausing along the way to rob a filling station, a hardware store, and a tavern. The filling station supplied them with some money and oil, and they took a variety of guns and ammunition from the hardware store and two cases of cheap whiskey from the tavern.

All of the thefts were reported to the state police, but few if any clues as to the identity of the thieves were available. The pair continued north, passing through Coconino when they left the main highway for a side trip into the mountains. In the high country they broke into a deserted fire guard station and set up housekeeping there for nearly a week. They devoted most of this time to target practice with the stolen guns and with drinking the stolen whiskey. Twice they came back to Coconino for groceries. They aroused Bud Stacy's curiosity when they tried to trade him a case of oil for a tank of gasoline.

"I knew they was out of line," Big Bud said later, nodding his bald head vigorously. "The little one did the talking whilst the tall one just stood there with the case of oil. The little one kept arguing while the tall one stood back and never even set the case down. I told 'em no. Told 'em I'd sell 'em all the gas they wanted, but no trade. I buy all my oil bulk. Got no use for those cans. Why, if I used quart cans I'd be all the time going to the dump. I got enough trash to get rid of as it is."

But, of course, Bud had spotted them as a pair of "baduns" and had spoken to Roscoe about them. Roscoe asked immediately if Bud had gotten their license number, and the big garageman had to admit that it had never occurred to him.

"First thing you want to do," Roscoe told him, "when you see something suspicious is get the plate number."

Bud said that Roscoe had gotten out the tattered sheaf of mimeographed lists of stolen cars which the county sheriff had left with him nearly six months earlier. There did not seem to be anything answering the description of the gray coupe listed there, but Roscoe kept the list out on the desk in the garage office where he made his headquarters and told Bud to be sure and let him know if the two men turned up again.

The unholy pair withdrew to the cabin in the hills again where they applied themselves to the whiskey and somehow convinced themselves that a large payroll was about to be delivered to the post office in Coconino.

When the townspeople learned about it afterwards, they

were amazed. Both of the lumber mills near town had been shut down for years. The loggers and lumbermen had long ago moved away, leaving behind the abandoned skeletons of their trade to rust and decay. The railroad did not pay off here. There were no industries. There was no bank. But the fact remains that the two young men believed that a considerable amount of money was about to be delivered to the post office and they made plans to steal it. After several days of planning and drinking, they loaded the stolen rifles, shotguns and pistols, finished off one more bottle of whiskey, and drove back to town.

It was a fine spring day and by noon had warmed considerably. Roscoe was on hand when "the girls" came over to open the post office as usual and told them to call him at Bud's if the morning train brought in anything that might require his help. The last either of them saw of him was as he crossed the wide main street to Mrs. Gowan's coffee shop.

This was one of Roscoe's regular stops because Mrs. Gowan opened earlier than anyone else in town in order to make the few breakfasts that she sold each day to single men like Bud Stacy who did not live at Mrs. Brady's; and since hers was the only light on Main Street, the early bus dropped off its daily load of morning papers at her door.

By the time Roscoe arrived she would have her version of the day's headlines well rehearsed and would deliver them with a cup of coffee to "the Constable." Mrs. Gowan was a widow and knowledgeable in regard to masculine egos as well as appetites. She was a small but robust woman of prodigious activity and immense vitality. She had cooked for her "regulars" so long that they hardly needed bother ordering. Moving up and down behind the little counter, she had a word for each of them, asked about their aches or ailments, admonished them to eat their vegetables, opened her brown eyes wide at their remarks and spiced her meals with her personality. She always referred to and addressed Roscoe as "Constable," just as she called Pete Nichols, who was a captain of cavalry in World War I, "Colonel."

Roscoe stopped in for coffee as usual that morning, and they discussed the day's news. Her breakfast rush was over and she was glad to draw up a stool across the counter from him and join him with a cup. There had been a shooting in Prescott the day before which they discussed. This led them to the subject of guns.

Mr. Gowan had been very fond of guns and hunting. She thought that became a man, but she herself was afraid of weapons of all kinds. She had given away all of Mr. Gowan's guns shortly after his death. Roscoe told her about his father's pistol which he had. Didn't have any cartridges for it, he said, because it was an old black powder caliber which they didn't make any more, but the gun was in fine shape. He would bring it up and show it to her. The conversation shifted, and he left for Bud's "to see if there had been any calls."

Bud Stacy says that Roscoe arrived " 'bout his usual time." They talked over the Prescott shooting, and it turned out that Bud knew one of the men involved. There had been no "calls," there seldom were any, but Roscoe said that maybe the sheriff in Prescott might want to know if either of the men involved in the shooting had been seen previously in Coconino drinking or arguing.

At noon Roscoe left for dinner at Mrs. Brady's, and he was back an hour or so later. Bud had then gone for his midday meal at Mrs. Gowan's and had gone all over the shooting again, explaining which of the men it was that he had known. He was surprised when he returned to the garage to find Roscoe cleaning a pistol at his desk.

"It was a old single-action Frontiersman," Bud said. "A forty-four-forty like they used to make so a man could shoot the same ammunition in his rifle and pistol. I told Roscoe I knew where he could get some cartridges to fit it. There's a fellow up to Flag that loads all kinds of shells. But the old boy said he didn't want none. Didn't aim to do any shooting. Just kept the gun on account of it being his dad's."

They had been sitting in the office talking about guns when the phone rang at about two-thirty. Roscoe answered, and Bud could hear the voice on the other end of the line "squawking excited like."

"What's up?" Bud asked.

"Something going on at the post office," Roscoe said and started out the door.

It was then that Bud noticed that the old man was wearing the gunbelt and holster.

"It's funny," he said later, "but there was something about the way it hung on him. Natural and easy. The shiny old handle of the Colt sticking up where it was handy. Seeing him wearing a gun didn't surprise me like it should. He looked like he wore it all the time and wouldn't look right without it."

Why hadn't he gone with Roscoe? Did he suspect trouble?

"Hell, no. He was always getting called up to the post office. Them girls called him to fix everything. Roscoe never said anything. Just walked right out. Turned out this was one thing he couldn't fix."

At about two o'clock a woman with vivid red hair (obviously dyed), wearing pedal pushers (obviously a tourist), entered the little wooden post office and spent a few minutes at the counter opposite the stamp window scribbling messages on an assortment of picture postcards. Martha was seated at a desk behind the partition, which divides the post office, adding up receipts, and Jenny waited at the stamp window, peering out between the bars of the grill, while the red-haired tourist finished the cards. She knew that the woman would want stamps.

As she waited she was thinking to herself that she could probably come very close to guessing the messages on the backs of the colorful cards without reading them after they were dropped in the slot. While the tourist was still writing, a tall young man with long flax-colored hair which he wore combed straight back and unparted came in from the street. He glanced at Jenny and then at the red-haired woman and hesitated. Then he stepped to the counter-desk and took a money-order blank from the rack along the wall and started writing. Both he and the woman had their backs toward Jenny for several minutes.

She noticed that the young man was wearing khaki pants which were badly in need of washing and an army field jacket which he had buttoned despite the warm afternoon. When the woman turned and took the single step which brought her from the desk to Jenny's window, the young man put down his pen and studied what he had written. Jenny busied herself issuing the required stamps and making change.

She heard the door open from the street but did not look in that direction until the woman had smiled and turned away, and then it was simply to watch the well-filled pedal pushers waggle back out into the sunlight. She noticed that another young man, this one small and dark with close-cropped hair, had joined the tall blond at the desk and they were murmuring together. She waited. The blond one stepped toward her, and the smaller man moved toward the front door.

The next thing she knew she was staring into the muzzle of a pistol which had been thrust at her through the bars of the grill, and the blond was saying something but all she heard was "stick up." The door in the partition burst open, and the small dark one came straight toward her leveling another pistol. Jenny gasped, thinking Martha will look up and scream her silly head off and they will become frightened and shoot us both.

But Martha did not scream. She sucked in her breath audibly but made no other sound. The blond one came through to the forbidden side of the partition and both men were talking at once. Jenny heard the words "money ... payroll ... safe ... hurry."

It didn't make sense to her because they seldom had over a hundred dollars on hand. The men kept jabbering about a big payroll.

The dark-haired youth shouted up into Jenny's dead-white face and the smell of whiskey slapped her like a blow with a bar towel. The blond stepped back, and the shorter man raised his pistol and clubbed her a glancing blow on the side of the head. She staggered back against a desk, but did not fall.

Her ears were ringing and everything was out of focus, but she was still conscious.

Martha, timid little Martha who is afraid to even pick out her own clothes, stepped directly up to the two armed men, shouting, "Leave her alone, you bullies!!" It may have been that this shout carried faintly across the street to Mrs. Gowan's and attracted her attention, she is not sure why she looked over at the post office just then, but she did just in time to see through the wide, single-paned window two men on the wrong side of the partition struggling with one of "the girls." One glimpse was all she got, and then the figures moved away toward the rear of the building.

Mrs. Gowan did not hesitate. She took a coin from the elaborately scrolled cash register and walked straight back to the pay phone attached to the back wall of the café. She dialed the number of Bud Stacy's garage, heard the phone ring twice at the other end, and recognized Roscoe's "Hello."

"There's something funny going on over at the post office, Constable," she said. "This is Jewel Gowan and I just saw some men through the window. They're in the back part and it looked to me like they were being rough with one of the Moore girls."

"Be right there," Roscoe said and hung up.

Mrs. Gowan hung up and returned to the window where all she could see was the battered gray coupe parked directly in front of the post office door. She watched the window but could not see far enough into the interior to see the two men ransacking the place, pulling out drawers and dumping their contents out on the floor. Jenny half sat and half leaned on the desk where she had wound up after being clubbed. Martha watched the dark-haired man paw through the drawers and cabinets. "There isn't any money," she kept insisting.

"Shut her up, will you?" the dark one snarled at the taller youth, who did not move.

"Goddamit," the dark one shouted, "have you lost your guts or something?"

The blond seemed to try to rouse himself but still did

not move, so the shorter of the two robbers grabbed Martha roughly by her arm and shoved her into the little lavatory and locked the door on her.

"Now go out to the car," the dark one said. "Go out and keep anyone from coming in. I'll sweat the truth out of this one. What's the matter with you? Move. Can't you even do a simple thing like that? Just go out and sit in the car and make sure nobody comes in, for Crissake."

Mrs. Gowan saw the tall blond come out and climb into the gray coupe. She could not make out what he was doing. She saw Roscoe crossing toward the little white building trimmed in green. As the old cowboy stepped up onto the low porch a few feet from the front door she saw a movement in the car, heard a loud report and saw Roscoe jackknife as he was hurled back into the dusty road. Another report sounded and she saw splinters fly from the wall. She was paralyzed with surprise.

The door to the post office slammed open, and the shorter man rushed out onto the porch. He looked down at Roscoe and then flung himself into the coupe, pushing his companion away from the wheel. The car roared to life and leaped away from the porch as doors opened up and down the street. Two more blasts made Jake Harmon, the barber, and Bud Stacy jump back to cover.

When they looked out again the car was gone. Jenny was screaming from the post office steps, Martha was hammering on the lavatory door inside, Mrs. Gowan was hurrying across the wide street and Roscoe was lying dead half on, half off the porch.

He had been hit just above the belt with a charge from a fully-cocked twenty-gauge shotgun at a distance of about fifteen feet. The pattern of the shot had not opened up and it almost cut him completely in two. The second shot left a hole about as big around as a softball in the outer wall of the building just a few inches above the floor line.

For a few minutes all was confusion. People rushed up the street, women screamed and men shouted, Jenny fainted and the two men who lifted Roscoe to the porch floor turned away quickly and vomited in the dusty street. Someone heard Martha pounding and kicking at the door inside and let her out. She rushed to the porch where almost the entire town was pushing and milling and pointing.

"Go after them! Go after them!" she shouted. "They robbed the post office."

"That ain't all," Bud Stacy growled. "They killed old Roscoe."

"Get them, Bud," Martha sobbed, "catch the brutes."

Big Bud Stacy surprised everyone then. They had all thought of him up until that time as a fat, lazy braggart who loafed around his garage telling lies about his prowess, who did consistently sloppy work, who complained constantly and who eyed young girls, licking his lips lecherously. Big Bud strode out into the street away from the crush and shouted for attention. Everyone looked toward him. He stood there in the dust with his tree-trunk legs spread wide apart, his arms raised.

"Get your cars," he shouted, "get your guns. We'll go after them. They headed east."

The crowd roared approval and surged away from the post office toward their homes, cars, pickups, and guns. Martha grasped Bud's sleeve.

"They can't turn off before Big Springs," she said. "Call Harvey Lacey at Parker Meadow. They'll have to pass there and he can stop them."

Bud stared in surprise at Martha for an instant, then whirled and loped across the street to Mrs. Gowan's where he telephoned Lacey at his filling station-store forty-five miles east of Coconino. By taking the road east out of town the killers had no choice but to pass there because there were no side roads leading off the highway other than trails which led out into the rangeland to the south or up into the mountains in the north.

Cars and pickups were roaring out of town as Bud hurriedly told Lacey what had happened. Men with deer rifles, shotguns, and pistols scurried about the street shouting and waving to one another. Bud slammed down the receiver and started out the door.

"Call the sheriff, call the state cops," he barked at Mrs. Gowan who was just coming in.

A station wagon slid to a stop in front of him and he climbed in beside two other men. One of the men handed him a thirty-thirty saddle gun, and the car jumped away as Bud slammed the door.

Someone had started ringing the church bell, and it gave off a persistent but somewhat irregular alarm as the last of the cars left town, throwing up clouds of dirt as the spinning back wheels propelled them away from the curb.

Roscoe's body lay on the post office porch covered with a tarpaulin, Jenny had been revived and was seated at the counter in Mrs. Gowan's café while most of the women of the town made much over her. Martha was at the phone calling the police.

Jenny recited her version of what had happened. Her sleek dark hair, usually drawn tightly back against her head, was disordered, and her ordinarily calm hazel eyes glinted with near hysteria. Martha was talking calmly into the telephone.

At the eastern end of Main Street, where the town ends abruptly, giving way to sagebrush and junipers, Bud Stacy had ordered a roadblock set up in case the fugitives managed to double back. Five men had remained behind and backed two flatbed trucks together across the road. The men leaned against the trucks and squinted out across the range where the gray ribbon of road wound away like a lariat carelessly tossed to earth. They told the story again and again, with variations, and when they were joined by Roscoe's cronies from Mrs. Brady's the story was gone over once more.

It was nearly dark when the first of the police arrived. The sheriff, with four deputies, drove into town with a flourish. They were joined shortly by three carloads of state police in natty uniforms. After much radioing back and forth, the trucks were ordered off the pavement and three of the cars rushed down the highway headed east with orders from the burly state police sergeant to send all men from town home.

"They'll start shooting one another pretty soon," he said.

But they did not do any shooting. They found the gray coupe where it had been abandoned off in the brush and later the body of the tall blond youth where he had put the muzzle of one of the stolen pistols in his mouth and pulled the trigger. The shorter man was captured several days later by a search party.

They buried Roscoe Banks on Saturday, May 6, 1950, in the neat little cemetery on a hill just outside Coconino, Arizona. It was a pleasant day with a soft breeze coming off the mountains to the north, and the countryside was vivaciously green after a long winter. The odor of freshly dug earth mingled with the sharp scent of the cedars. As the smooth-cheeked young parson intoned the ritual some of the women pressed handkerchiefs to their eyes with little dabbing motions. Some of the men peered intently at nothing in the distance. Those who had known him best thought about Roscoe and the others simply let their minds go blank, giving themselves up to solemnity.

"Here was a man," the preacher said, "whose like few of us will ever see again. Here was a man whose virtues were integrity, responsibility, and an abiding code of personal honor.

"Here was a man."